LITTLE MAN

LITTLE MAN

by elizabeth mann

MIKAYA PRESS

NEW YORK

BOOKS BY ELIZABETH MANN

The Brooklyn Bridge
The Great Pyramid
The Great Wall
The Roman Colosseum
The Panama Canal
Machu Picchu
Hoover Dam
Tikal
Empire State Building
The Parthenon
Taj Mahal
Statue of Liberty

Copyright © 2014 Mikaya Press

Editor: Stuart Waldman
Design: Lesley Ehlers Design
Map: Lesley Ehlers

Distributed in North America by:
Firefly Books LTD, 50 Staples Ave.
Unit 1, Richmond Hill, Ontario, Canada L4B0A7

Cataloging-in-Publication Data
available from the Library of Congress

Printed in The United States of America

For Joanie and Brenda

The author wholeheartedly acknowledges the people who helped make *Little Man*. Draft after draft after draft, Joan Elizabeth Goodman and Brenda DeCommer were consistently smart, patient, rigorous and encouraging. Stu Waldman and Lucas Mann, as always, edited wisely. Sally Alexander and John Alexander read carefully and commented astutely. Amy Thurman and Sandra Jarett checked and double-checked. Charlie and the Sky Dancers inspired. Thanks, everyone.

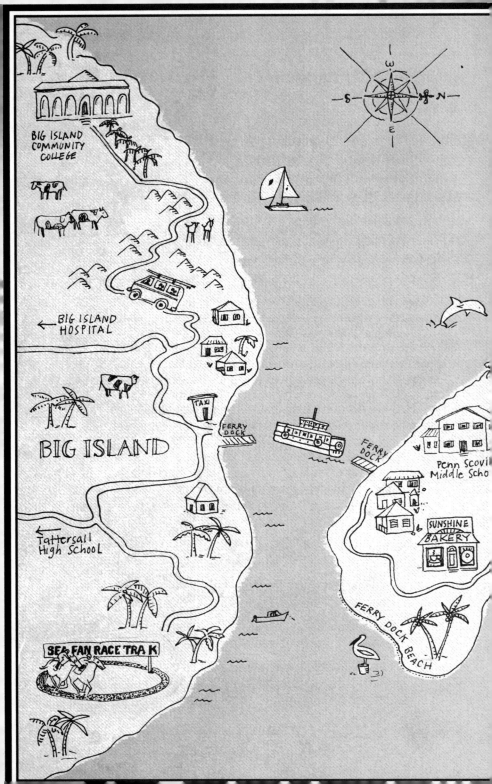

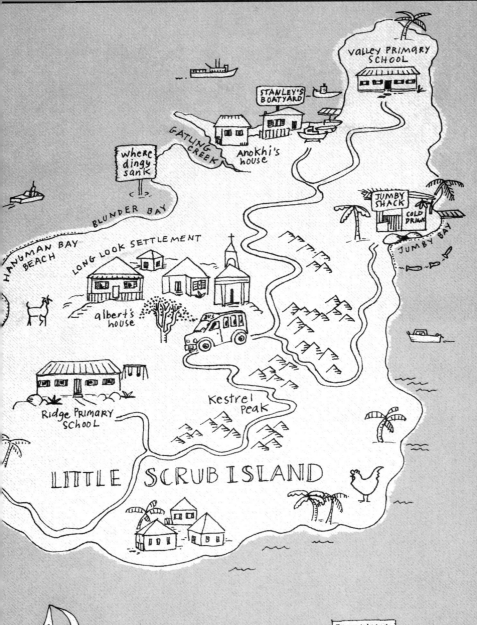

VALLEY PRIMARY SCHOOL

STANLEY'S BOATYARD

GATLING CREEK

where dingy sank

Anokhi's house

BLUNDER BAY

JUMBY SHACK
COLD DRINK

JUMBY BAY

HANUMAN BAY BEACH

LONG LOOK SETTLEMENT

albert's house

Kestrel Peak

Ridge Primary School

LITTLE SCRUB ISLAND

BROOKLYN 1631 MILES

1

Little Man

At first, the hollering seemed like part of his dream. In the dream, his father was yelling at him to wake up and get ready for the first day of middle school. But when he opened his eyes, his father was yelling at him to wake up and get ready for the first day of middle school. The neighbor's goats were bleating hungrily in their pen on the hillside below, the date palm fronds outside the window were clacking in the breeze, and he was sweating. This was no dream. More like a nightmare, a real live nightmare. He pulled the sheet over his head, but the yelling still came through loud and clear.

"Ashanti, Chente! Somebody wake up Albert! That bus'll be here any minute!" His brothers, already half-dressed, were happy to help. They towered over Albert, laughing, swinging pillows, and slinging insults until he had to scurry out of bed to escape them.

Albert began putting on his uniform. It was a hand-me-down from Ashanti's middle school days, and it looked like a hand-me-down. It looked worse than a hand-me-down. Ashanti, like Chente, had always been tall for his age. They took after Daddy. Mommy was five feet no inches tall, so anyone with eyes could see where Albert had gotten his height. Or his lack of height.

His father always said of Mommy: "Norma may be a little thing, but I sure want her on my side in a fight." Tiny but tough. His mother took care of business all right. Albert sometimes wished he had inherited more of the tough and less of the tiny.

As Albert buttoned the shirt, his stomach sank. Whatever else she was, his mother wasn't great with a needle. She had hemmed the sleeves and pant legs well enough, but making the uniform narrow enough for Albert was apparently beyond her. He tucked the shirt in and snugged the belt tight. The uniform ballooned out above and below it.

He stood on the bed to see himself in the little mirror, and his worst fears were confirmed. It was bad. Even with the top button buttoned, there was room for another thin little chicken neck inside the collar, and his Dumbo ears had never looked so huge. His mother had always told him he looked cute as a button in the oversized hand-me-downs he'd worn all his life, but now he wondered if maybe he'd been looking foolish all his life.

His brothers took his place at the mirror to tie the neckties that were required for high school. Albert watched as they concentrated on perfecting their knots and getting the two ends of their ties to just the right lengths. Big and tall and straight, they looked handsome even in the maroon and beige plaid shirts and maroon polyester pants that somebody somewhere decided was the just the right outfit to help high school students stay focused on their work in the classroom while the blue Caribbean Sea beckoned to them outside.

The middle school uniform, with its yellow shirt and brown pants, wasn't any better, but Albert remembered that even though Ashanti had hated it, he had managed to look cool when he wore it.

There had been a time when Albert had looked forward to middle school, to being big like Ashanti and looking cool in the yellow shirt like Ashanti. He still hadn't grown big like Ashanti, and looking cool like him was out of the question. And as far as middle school, Albert shook his head at the idea that he had ever looked forward to it. Right now there was nothing he dreaded more. He would rather swim into fire coral than go to middle school. He would rather work all day weeding Auntie Taggert's banana trees than go to middle school. He would rather . . .

"Come on, Albert! Quit staring into space. Mommy wants you to eat something before the bus gets here." Ashanti gave him one last whack.

"Ouch," Albert said, though the pillow hadn't hurt him at all.

The bus bounced over the potholes toward Albert as he stood miserably in the shade of the Sea Grape tree, the same place he had waited for the last five years for the bus that carried him and his best friend, Linden, from Long Look Settlement to Ridge Primary School. It wasn't a bus really, but a white van with three rows of seats behind the driver and no glass in any of the side windows. It was so packed with kids that when he dropped them off at their settlements in the afternoon, the driver, Mr. Frett, didn't bother to wait for them to climb over each other to get out the single side door. Instead he would get out, reach in through the windows, and pluck kids from their seats. Backpacks and all, he would swing them in a big arc high in the air and set them down, giggling, at their stop. Suddenly, Albert missed those strong arms more than he would have thought possible.

The middle school bus was nothing like Mr. Frett's van. It was a real school bus, yellow, like the one in *The Magic School Bus*, with glass in all the windows and black lettering on the back that said "School Bus No Passing." Albert knew about the black lettering because that was what he saw as the bus rattled right past him. He took off running after it, sleeves and pant legs flapping, yelling, "Hey! Hold up! Stop!"

The driver seemed nice enough when he opened the door, smiling down at Albert through the dust that puffed up from the tires where he had screeched to a halt, but when he greeted him he said, "Morning, morning, little man. You so small, I didn't even see you under that big tree."

Albert, too winded to speak, nodded as he pulled himself up the bus steps and walked into a wall of laughter—howling, out-of-control, tears-running-down-cheeks laughter. The bus was already half-full of kids—Stanley kids from Gatling Creek Settlement—and they had watched every second of Albert's frantic dash. He sank into the first empty seat and ducked his head.

His ears and cheeks burned as the raucous laughter settled into a more orderly, and more humiliating, chant: "Little Man, Little Man, you so small, didn't hardly see you at all."

The sprawling Stanley family owned the boat yard in Gatling Creek, and they only hired family to work there. Stanley kids, a jumble of siblings, half-siblings, and cousins, only played with each other, and they could be mean. Just last summer, a bunch of the boys had swarmed onto the Gatling Creek dock when Albert and Linden approached in their little dinghy. Big, funny Linden had made them laugh, though, softening the sting of their taunts and preventing things from turning nasty. Gatling Creek kids went to Valley Primary, so Albert rarely saw them, but since there was only one middle school on the island, he shouldn't have been surprised that they were on the bus. The realization that he would have to put up with them every day for the rest of the school year set his mind reeling.

"Little Man, Little Man . . ."

Albert recognized Silton Stanley's braying voice rising above the others in the back of the bus. Silton had been the ringleader on the dock that day. He was the biggest and the loudest, stomping around shirtless, flexing his muscles and threatening to sink the dinghy. He seemed to be the ringleader again today.

From the back of the bus, louder than ever, came, "Little Man, Little Man, you so small . . ."

Would it ever stop? Albert dug his fingernails into his palms and began his own, silent chant, "Can't cry, rather die. Can't cry, rather die." He wished Linden were with him. The bus lurched sharply to a stop at the side of the road. The driver slowly stood and turned to face the back. He wasn't tall, but he was solid, and he seemed to grow larger as he stood quietly surveying the bus. A couple of leftover sniggers escaped and then there was silence, blessed silence. The driver walked a few paces and stopped by Albert's seat. His big voice rumbled out, "You boys are vexing me for true. You save that foolishness for the playground."

A few voices protested lamely. "Aw, Peachy, come on, Mon. We didn't do anything! Take it easy!" Albert winced, even more embarrassed at being defended, but at least the chanting didn't start again. As Peachy turned to go back to his seat, his hand rested briefly on Albert's shoulder. It was a kind touch, and Albert's eyes stopped smarting. He straightened in his seat and looked out the window. The bus came to the end of the switchback curves on the hillside and picked up speed as it turned onto the level coast road. The Caribbean sparkled in the bright morning sun. Albert used to think the sea was winking at him when the light glinted on it. Of course, he didn't think that anymore, but he still liked it when the sun and water played like that.

Three pelicans, one after the other, made short, awkward, headfirst plunges smack into the water just as the bus went by. He almost smiled.

2

Middle School

Peachy turned left and pulled up behind the two buses already parked in the school's circular driveway, and the kids piled out and scattered. Albert hung back, checking out the cracked asphalt basketball court by the drive. There was a pickup game going on under each basketless rim, and the clang as the ball hit the metal backboard was the loudest sound of the morning. The players were big, but the games looked loose and not very serious. That was a good sign.

Albert edged closer to the edge of the court. He thought about Ashanti, how he would have jumped off the bus and gotten into a game like it was the easiest thing in the world. Maybe he should try to be more like Ashanti, get into the game. Yeah. Get into the game. If Linden were here, he would do it. If he was going to go to middle school, he should act like he was in middle school. Maybe. Maybe starting tomorrow.

Albert was in the middle of his private pep talk when a

ball ricocheted high off the rim toward his face. He threw his hands up reflexively and caught it. It felt familiar between his palms, as worn and smooth as the old ball he and Linden used to use at Ridge Primary. Without thinking, he began dribbling. He thought he was a pretty good dribbler. He and Linden had spent hours practicing their moves. Even Ashanti said they looked professional. Almost professional.

He dribbled fast and low toward the basket, looked up to aim his shot, and got the shock of his life. The basket was a mile above his head! He stumbled but managed to fling the ball toward it anyway. It hit the pole below the backboard and rolled away onto the dry, brown grass. For the second time that morning, Albert's cheeks and ears heated up as laughter rippled over him. It took about a nanosecond for Silton to appear beside the court and bring the bus chant back to life in a new form.

"Little Man, Little Man, you so small. You can't hardly shoot at all!" Albert tried to act like he was in on the joke by giving a little hands-up shrug as he walked off the court. It was a weak attempt, but he was too stunned to care. He had to think.

In middle school, the baskets were higher than the ones at Ridge Primary! How come he didn't know that? Gatling Creek kids went to middle school. What else didn't he know? In the shade of the aluminum awning that sagged over the front door, he studied the hand-lettered "Welcome New Students" sign as though he were going to be tested on it. What was waiting for him on the other side of that door?

During first-period homeroom, Mr. Shipley called the roll.

"Quashie? Albert Quashie? Oh, there you are. Quashie. From Long Look Settlement? Is Ashanti your family?"

"Yes, sir. He's my brother."

"And Chente too? Fine athletes. I didn't know we had more Quashies coming up so soon. We can sure use someone to replace Ashanti. What sports do you play, Albert?"

"Not basketball!" came the whisper from behind him, followed by a sputter of smothered laughter. Mr. Shipley instantly turned his attention to crushing the little outbreak. He forgot about Albert. Whew.

"Is something funny? Settle down immediately. A week in detention is a very bad way to start out in middle school."

Albert kept his eyes fixed on his hands on the battered desktop. He laced his fingers together so tightly they hurt, and tried to make sense of this latest surprise. In middle school, people expected him to be like Ashanti! How come he didn't know that? Of course, he knew that Ashanti was the man. Who didn't? Cricket, basketball, everything, he was the star. Albert was prouder of him than anyone, but there was no way he could fill those big, athletic shoes. Slamdunking a ball through that hoop outside would be easier. Albert had been short for his age for a long time, but he had never felt so small.

Homeroom was an extended period on the first day, and it seemed to extend forever. When it finally ended,

Albert sighed out loud with relief. He had survived, and there had been no more surprises. Out in the corridor, the jostling and noise somehow made him feel better. He wasn't smiling, and he sure wasn't laughing, but least he wasn't fighting not to cry.

A trickle of students broke off from the main stream, and he flowed with them into his next class. Maths. If there was one thing he was good at it was Maths. Every June, his mother added more blue Maths Achievement ribbons to the dusty row tacked over his bed. Just thinking about his pencil skittering across a page, trying to keep up as his mind solved the problems, could make him happy.

The Maths teacher was a small, round woman in a dark blue dress. Her tiny face peered out from the puff of gray hair that framed it. The flesh of her neck wobbled like a pelican's pouch when she spoke. He smiled at the thought of the look Linden would have given if he'd been there. She looked like someone's granny. He was pretty sure she was someone's granny, so he settled a polite expression on his face and prepared to let his mind drift as he'd learned to do when Granny Quashie began talking about her church. But instead of drifting off, he found himself straining to hear her.

"In this class, we are mathematicians," she said. "We think like mathematicians. We challenge ourselves like mathematicians with new problems, harder problems."

Albert liked the sound of that. This could be good. He fished a pencil out of his backpack. He was ready for a challenge. Maybe it would be adding hard fractions, like

17/18 plus 5/9 plus 3 8/33, or long division with decimals, like 29,438.45 divided by 316.427. Maybe she'd do word problems like the puzzlers in the *Mad Mad Maths* magazine he received for his last birthday. Two trains leave the station at the same time—he liked those.

"Even mathematicians sometimes forget things during the summer. Let's go back and see what you remember from Level 6 about quadratic equations." The flesh of her upper arm wobbled and danced as she wrote on the blackboard. Albert leaned to the side and nearly slipped off his chair trying to peer around her stout figure so he could start copying the problem.

She stepped away from the board, briskly dusting the chalk off her hands.

$$X (Y + X) = XY + XX$$

Huh? Albert stared at the white scratchings, trying to find something familiar. There were multiplication signs, but five of them? There were a couple of plus signs and an equals sign, but where were the numbers? What were those *Y*s doing there? Was quadratic some kind of secret code?

"What can you tell me about this equation?" Tentative hands went up around the room. The code must not be so secret if everyone else knew it. Albert slid down in his seat and ducked his head, trying to make himself as invisible as possible. Another surprise. Just because he skipped Level 6 didn't mean he knew everything that was taught that year! How had he not realized that? When his teacher called his parents in to talk about having him skip Level 6 and go right into First Form in middle school, he felt as smart as a superhero. Now he felt as dumb as a box of rocks.

"Hi, hi, Albert. How was school today?"

Albert looked up from the bench in the shady corner of the deck at the back of the house, where he was leaning against the faded blue wall. He had opened his Earth Science book half an hour earlier but hadn't gotten past the table of contents. His mother was all smiles and interest. She sat down next to him and opened the brown, butter-stained bag that she always brought home from Sunshine Bakery. Today it was Teacher Elma's Honey Loaf Cake with Walnuts. They each took a slice and munched in silence.

"Now, Albert, how was school?" This time her voice had a little extra sound, a worried sound. He could tell that his silence was getting to her, but where could he start? The bus ride? "Little Man, Little Man?" The science teacher who lined up students by height? Sitting alone in the lunchroom?

Linden would never have left him alone in the lunchroom. No matter what anyone said, Linden would have sat with him. If Linden had climbed onto the school bus with him, the teasing would never have happened. The whole day would have been different. But Linden was in Brooklyn, and he wouldn't be back for a whole year. Maybe never, if his father liked teaching there more than he liked teaching at Big Island Community College. Albert still couldn't understand why The Professor wanted to teach Caribbean Studies in America instead of the Caribbean, especially since it meant that his best friend had to go too. Big, funny Linden with his fake karate kicks and his wild, splashy way of swimming and his crazy plan to sell skateboards on their hilly little island where half the roads weren't even paved, and his . . .

"Albert?"

"Hey, remember when me and Linden salvaged that old dinghy that sank after Hurricane Frieda? And remember we took it out into Blunder Bay and it started to leak?" This adventure, like many of their dinghy adventures, had become a family legend. No matter how often it was told, people would still laugh and interrupt with their own versions of what had happened when the fishing boat arrived to rescue the boys and who had said what when they were pulled out of the water. This was much safer than talking about school, and Albert was all set to launch into the story, but his mother wasn't having any of it.

She interrupted him. "Did you miss having Linden with you today?"

He took a breath. "A little. Yeah." His mother seemed to already know what kind of a day he'd had. Talking about it would just make him cry and make her worry. He had to get out of this.

"But not really. School was okay. My Maths teacher is weird. She's a lady but she's got a mustache. For true, no fooling. And hairs in her nose too. For true." His mother didn't press him further, and they fell into their old routine. Since kindergarten, he had come home doing funny imitations of his teachers, the way they stood and spoke and held their teacups. When he started on Mrs. Scatliffe in Maths, his mother responded with her usual mixture of laughing and scolding. The laughter egged him on, but she always had the last word.

"Albert, it's a good thing you have a kind heart. I know you would never be funny to hurt." He did his imitations only at home. Or for Linden.

The phone rang and his mother went inside. She would be busy for a while now. It was one thing to be miserable, but it was another, far worse thing to see his mother sad on his account. It was bad enough that she already knew he was too ashamed of his first day to talk about it. At least he hadn't cried. He opened his Earth Science book and found the assignment page—clouds. That seemed easy enough. Maybe he could be good in Earth Science since he wasn't good at Maths anymore.

3

Saturday Night

A week went by, and then another. School hadn't gotten any better, and Albert had resigned himself to the slow creep of time from Monday to Friday. What he would never get used to was how the weekends crawled by. That had never happened before. He and Linden always had so much to do that their families called them the Busy Busy Boys. He shifted his weight on the bench. He had never sat on the porch on Saturdays before, but everything was different without Linden. He tried to think about being busy, busy, but there wasn't anything he wanted to do. His family had stopped asking "Why are you always sitting around?", so he didn't look up at the hollow sound of his father's footsteps, figuring that he was heading for his big wicker "king" chair to look at the sea. Instead, the footsteps stopped and his father's long legs folded as he sat down next to Albert. Something was up.

"Hi, hi, Albert."

"Hi, hi, Daddy."

"Schoolwork?" He pointed at the book Albert was reading.

"Nah. This is that Harry Potter book The Professor gave me before they left."

"Oh. Uh-huh. Uh-huh." There was a pause. Something was definitely up.

"Albert, I'll be needing your help." Uh-oh. Daddy was using his "time to clean the gutters" voice. But hadn't he just done it? Surely it was Ashanti's turn, or Chente's, or somebody's. Albert hated that chore. Just thinking about climbing the ladder tied his stomach into a knot.

When Albert turned eleven, Daddy said he was old enough to help with cleaning gutters, the most important chore in the house. When Albert froze at the foot of the ladder, Daddy said the best way for him to handle his fear of heights was to climb up the ladder. Albert had said the best way to handle his fear was to stay off the ladder, since he was only afraid when he was on it.

Daddy said, in his deepest voice, that if leaves blocked the gutters, rainwater couldn't get to the cistern, and the family could run out of drinking water. Fear of a water shortage got Albert up the ladder that first time, but he wasn't looking forward to a second.

"I'll need you to tote equipment tonight."

What? Albert started to speak but couldn't. He swallowed hard, twice, and finally said, "Uh, tote equipment? Tonight?"

"The band's playing tonight."

"The band's playing? Tonight?"

Daddy chuckled. "Albert, is there an echo out here or did some Jumby come along and turn you into a parrot?"

Daddy and his band, the Orion Stars, had been playing for as long as Albert could remember at a beach bar called the Jumby Shack on the north side of the island. During the day, it was a sleepy place where a handful of fishermen gathered after they'd unloaded the morning's catch and cleaned their boats. But every so often, on a Saturday night, it became the most popular place on the island. A pig roast barbecue and the Orion Stars attracted crowds. And it wasn't just Little Scrub Island folks. Tourists on passing sailboats, people from other islands, everybody came, and the dancing went on until late. On those certain Saturday nights, the Jumby Shack became a very dangerous place. At least that's what Albert's mother told him and Linden every time they begged to go along with Daddy and the band. She had never been to a Jumby Shack pig roast barbecue, and she wasn't about to let any child of hers run around on a dark beach crowded with strangers. Even Ashanti had never been.

"But Daddy, but . . . You mean . . . ? But what about . . . ?"

"What? Mommy? She's cool."

"But . . . but . . . why . . . ?"

"Now if you don't want to go . . ."

"No! I mean yes, Daddy, sure, yeah, sure! Yes, I want to go!" Out of nowhere the rule was gone. It was very confusing, but at least he wasn't going to be cleaning gutters. He was going to the Jumby Shack on a Saturday night. If only Linden were coming too.

"Go on, start pulling things out of the shed. Red Dog and them'll be here soon, soon," Daddy said. Albert jumped to his feet but noticed his mother in the window that opened to the porch. She had been listening to every word Daddy said.

"Hey, Mommy, I don't get it."

"Baby, your daddy and I, we've watched you for a month now sitting quiet on that bench, so. Friday, Saturday, Sunday, just sitting. It's not like you, and we've been talking. I never thought I'd hear myself say such a thing to a child of mine, but I think maybe you need to get your nose out of the books, shake things up a little. I don't suppose just once will hurt. But you be careful! Stay close to the band. Keep away from strangers."

"Okay," said Albert. He paused before heading for the shed, trying to shake off a clammy feeling that was settling over his excitement. He didn't like his parents worrying about him like that. It made him feel different and weird. It was bad enough feeling that way at school, but at home too?

"Yeeeaggh!" He interrupted his thoughts with the karate scream that Linden had taught him as he leaped off the back deck. He karate chopped furiously at the leaves as he wove between the mango and lime trees in his mother's little garden. Forget different and weird. It was Saturday night, and he was going to the Jumby Shack with the band!

Red Dog was the band's lead singer, and Albert

thought he looked the part. The sharp angles of his face and his long, hooked nose made him look a little dangerous. He drove a pickup truck that was flashy, flashier than anything on the island. It was big and red and shiny, with leather seats front and back, fancy spinning rims on the wheels, and flames painted on the sides. A decal spelled out "Fast 'n' Furious" across the top of the windshield, and the powerful engine purred menacingly. But no matter how dangerous Red Dog and his truck appeared, nothing fast or furious ever happened when he was at the wheel.

Albert sat in the back seat next to Sammy, the band's drummer, who was tappity-tapping on his knees with his fingertips and accompanying himself with little clicky sounds in the back of his throat. He stopped clicking long enough to say, "Red Dog, my granny drives faster than you, and she's been dead for years."

Albert giggled. Linden would have loved this. The others chuckled, but Red Dog said nothing. He watched the road ahead and hummed softly along with the radio.

After a while he said, "I have to drive slow. You know I have to drive slow. You see these people?"

They were passing through a settlement and came to a group of beer drinkers who called out "hi, hi" to him from where they sat atop the stone wall outside Emo's bar. The wooden window shutters of the small lavender building were opened wide and Albert could see the empty white plastic chairs and the unused pool table inside. Everyone, even Emo himself, was outside enjoying the cooling breeze at the end of the day.

"You see Emo and Charlie and all of them?" said Red Dog. "You think they want this truck to speed by? They don't want this truck to speed by! They want a good long look at this pretty truck. I *have* to drive slow."

His passengers laughed, and Red Dog continued on at the same stately, deliberate speed around curves and between potholes as they climbed higher and higher up Kestrel Ridge. It reminded Albert of being on the Lions Club float during the last Emancipation Day parade, but with no crowds and no candy to throw. And no Linden. It seemed like every time he remembered something fun, it reminded him of Linden. He sighed and turned to look out the window.

When they came to the next settlement a frantic beep-beep-beep sounded behind them. Blue, the band's bass player and youngest member, had lost patience following them. He pulled his dusty, sand-colored jeep alongside Fast 'n' Furious when it stopped at a crossroad, leaned out his window and said,

"Red Dog, you drive slower'n my granny and she's dead."

They all laughed as the battered jeep swerved in front of them and beepity-beeped out of sight around a bend. Albert watched Red Dog as he turned to talk to Daddy. He was so cool. And it wasn't just the dreadlocks tied with a leather strap, or the gold earrings, or the slow way he spoke, although all those were very cool. Red Dog had been teased twice about his driving and it didn't bother him at all. He even seemed to enjoy it. That was cool. Albert tried to imagine himself laughing along with the teasing at school, answering back the way Red Dog might. Maybe he could say something like, "That's me: Little Man. Good things come in small packages."

Naw. He could never do it. If Red Dog said it it would sound cool, but he could never do it.

4

Jumby Shack

By the time they made their way down the ridge and arrived at Jumby Bay, the sun was hovering low over the water, splashing the sky with a hundred shades of pink and lavender. The Jumby Shack squatted at one end of the beach. It was a shabby patchwork of wood and tin and canvas, but in the evening light it looked almost beautiful. Christmas lights glowed along the roof and on nearby palm tree trunks and along the dock further down the beach. Lights from sailboats anchored in the bay reflected in long, wiggly bands on the water. A breeze carried barbecue smells and laughter to where Albert stood next to Fast 'n' Furious, but it was the color of the sky that hypnotized him. He felt as though he'd never seen a sunset before.

He could have stood there forever, but Red Dog drawled, "I'm with you, Mon. I like grinning at the sky a whole lot more than I like toting amps, but I sent all my servants home early, so it looks like I'll be toting tonight."

Albert got the hint and moved to grab the other side of

the big keyboard case that Red Dog was pulling from the bed of the truck.

"What are you so happy about anyway?"

"Nothing," said Albert automatically. Wait, that wasn't true. He tried again.

"Everything."

He really did feel happy! And just a day ago, even two hours ago, he was looking out at the world from the bottom of a deep, dark hole. Now here he was grinning at the sky. Maybe he was different and weird.

The evening tumbled on. People he'd known forever and people he'd never seen before bumped his fist and rubbed his head when Red Dog told them he was the band's new roadie. When he tired of saying that school was okay and he didn't know where Ashanti was, he slipped away from the growing crowd to the jumble of massive granite boulders on the beach beside the Jumby Shack. The boulders looked as though a giant had tossed a handful of them carelessly on the sand. He clambered to the top of the biggest one and found the dent, like a giant's thumbprint, that he and Linden had found the time Red Dog bought lunch for them at the Jumby Shack. The stone was still warm from the day's sun, and he curled into the dent to watch the last of the sunset.

Suddenly, just as the sun slipped below the horizon, there it was! A green flash! He had seen a green flash once before when he and Linden were dragging homeward after a long day of fishing. They thought it was a message from aliens looking for friendly earthlings and raced home with the good news. He knew now that a green flash was just a rare trick of the light that happens when sky and water conditions were just right during a Caribbean sunset. But he felt as thrilled as he had then.

"You see that, Albert?" Daddy had come up and was standing on the beach next to his boulder.

"Yeah, Daddy! You too? That was so cool. Remember that time when me and Linden went fishing at Josiah's Bay and we saw the flash?"

"Oh, I remember. You two kept saying Martians were signaling you. I thought Chente and Ashanti would never stop laughing."

"Aw, come on, we were just kids. We didn't know."

His father stretched his long arm to hand a bottle up to him. Albert reached down to take it. The glistening bottle was the same green as the flash.

"Ting! Thanks, Daddy."

He took a gulp of the tart grapefruit soda. Albert loved Ting, but his mother didn't allow soda in the house. They watched the sky in silence as it kaleidoscoped through darker colors.

After a while, Daddy said, "Don't fill up on that stuff, Albert. You want to save room for Miss Serena's roast pig."

At the barbecue table, they heaped their paper plates full and joined the rest of the band at one of the big, wooden cable spools that the Jumby Shack used as beach tables. Albert polished off barbecued fish and ribs, cole slaw, macaroni pie, and Johnny cakes as well as two helpings of roast pig. Then he went back for a big slice of coconut cake. Stuffed, he left the table and went back to his boulder to digest and wait for the music to begin.

When Albert jerked awake, it was dark and he wasn't sure where he was. Then he heard music and remembered—he was at the Jumby Shack with Daddy. He stood up and stretched. The band was in a blaze of spotlight on the low plywood stage. The musicians curled over their instruments as they played, and the tendons in Red Dog's neck stood out as he stretched to sing into the microphone. They sounded good! The dance floor, a concrete slab on the sand, was packed with people, bobbing and swaying. The song ended, the dancers applauded, and Albert sat back down in the giant's thumbprint to listen, shivering a little against the cooling stone.

But what was this? Daddy unclipped the neck strap and leaned his bass guitar against a speaker. The calypso music was turned on again, the lights on the stage went out, and the band turned into dark silhouettes. Albert stood up, ready to jump off the boulder. If the show was over, he didn't want the band to leave without him. But no one seemed to be going anywhere, and the air was buzzing with excited talk.

He decided that the band was probably taking an early break, and that he was probably imagining the buzz in the air. He knew his imagination wasn't like when he was little and thinking up aliens, but still sometimes it was a little wild. He lay back on the boulder. It was a clear night, no moon, and the sky was matted with stars. The constellations got brighter as he peered into the black sky. He smiled when he found the three stars of Orion's Belt, and then the rest of Orion, the hunter. It was Mommy's favorite constellation, the first one she taught to Albert, the reason why the band was called the Orion Stars.

The sound system crackled annoyingly and the calypso music clicked off. More crackling, then loud funk music came on. Albert had never heard the song, but he liked its jumping bass beat. The spotlights blinked on again, washing the waiting dancers in light so bright that they raised their arms against the glare.

The sudden light hurt Albert's eyes too, and he looked away from it into darkness at the end of the beach. His eyes stopped hurting, but they began playing tricks on him. The palm trees by the dock looked like they were moving. Then they really were moving. Then they turned into shadowy giants. He tried to blink the shadows away, but they didn't disappear. They were still there, and they were moving fast toward the Jumby Shack. Should he shout a warning?

❧ 5 ❧

Mocko Jumbies

Before he could think, the swift-moving shadows stepped into the circle of light and changed instantly from dark shadows into brilliantly colored stiltwalkers. Mocko Jumbies! Of course! Albert felt a little sheepish, but still he shivered with excitement. It reminded him of the first time he and Linden saw Mocko Jumbies at an Emancipation Day Parade years before. At first, Albert was alarmed by the giant stiltwalkers, but then Linden told him they were Mocko Jumbies and he was scared witless. Daddy's most terrifying bedtime stories were about Jumbies.

Linden wasn't scared—he knew all about Mocko Jumbies from his father. Linden and The Professor managed to convince Albert that the *Mocko* Jumbies from Trinidad who walked on stilts in parades were not the same as the mean, evil, magic *Jumbies* in the stories. Still, the tingling goosebumps had lingered on Albert's arms, and now he had goosebumps all over again. Mocko Jumbies always gave him a thrill.

The crowd crushed back to make room, and the stilt-walkers exploded into action on the dance floor. High above the upturned faces of the audience, their dark arms moved like whips. The stilts never stopped moving, and their bodies, tiny above the long wooden legs, swayed like palm fronds. The stilts' tips tapped delicately as goats' hooves on the concrete slab. The yards of silky cloth of every color that draped the long stilt legs fluttered and shimmered in the spotlights.

If only Linden could see this! The stiltwalkers who danced along the parade route waving and bowing were nothing like this. These Mocko Jumbies were wild! One leaned so far backward that the crowd screamed in happy terror that he would fall, and then he sprung upright as if nothing had happened. One stepped onto a tabletop and danced without knocking over a single glass. Another teetered on one leg, arms flailing, pretending he was about to fall on the people flinching below him. It was as though they tried to outdo one another in the danger of their tricks.

They saved their most dangerous stunt for the end. Each stiltwalker kicked a stilt high out behind, and at the same time reached forward and grabbed the raised stilt of the person in front. When everyone was holding a stilt, they formed a circle, and they stood for a moment hopping in place. Then they began to hop forward, and the circle started to turn. They hopped faster, and the circle started to spin like a wheel. Albert could barely breathe. It was wild and dangerous, but through it all the Mocko Jumbies' faces remained still and expressionless, as remote and fabulous as the stars.

After the applause faded, the stiltwalkers beckoned, and the human-size dancers rushed to join them on the dance floor, dodging between their legs. Everybody was dancing, and every so often a Mocko Jumby would lean down, catch a pair of upstretched hands, and lift someone, usually a small woman, high into the air while the crowd laughed and clapped. Albert was on his feet too, dancing on top of his boulder.

One of the Mocko Jumbies left the dance floor and headed straight toward Albert's boulder. The long legs swallowed the distance between them, and in an instant the fluttering red and yellow trousers were so close that Albert could have touched them if he dared. Instead, he slowly raised his eyes to the face above. The sight of the bright blue Afro wig, black-lipsticked lips, and enormous mirrored sunglasses gave him a fresh tingle. Speechless, he stared at his own warped reflection in the sunglasses.

The Mocko Jumby's severe face split into a wide smile, and he reached his hands out. Albert caught them without hesitating and suddenly he was flying through the air. Before he even had a chance to worry about his arms popping out of their sockets, the giant had set him down lightly on the concrete. And before he even had a chance to feel embarrassed, he was dancing along with everyone else.

Too soon it was over. The Mocko Jumbies bowed, waved, and giant-stepped down the beach, disappearing into the dark. Albert, breathing hard, watched as the night swallowed them, then retreated back to his boulder. The Orion Stars came back on stage, and Red Dog stepped to the microphone.

"Thank you, Cloud Chasers!" he bellowed. "Everybody put your hands together one more time for the amazing Cloud Chasers! Our own Cloud Chasers!"

As the cheering faded, Daddy and the rest of the band stepped back onto the stage to finish their set. Albert listened to the music but didn't really hear them. Mocko Jumbies at the Jumby Shack! How come he never knew about that? Cloud Chasers! How come he never heard of them? At the end of the set, Albert jumped down from the boulder and ran over to the band.

"Daddy! Daddy! Those Cloud Chasers! They were so great! I never saw anything like that!"

"Well, I guess there was no band playing here tonight after all," grumbled Red Dog. His stare pinned Albert like a bug. His voice, heavy with hurt, dropped lower, a graveside voice.

"I thought there was a band playing here tonight, but maybe I was wrong, since some people didn't seem to notice any music," Red Dog said.

Albert squirmed. Red Dog had sung his heart out, and he'd acted like he hadn't heard. Albert hadn't meant to hurt his feelings, and he felt terrible.

"Hey, Red Dog, Mon, I sure heard you. Sorry. I'm sorry. You sounded amazing! For true! The whole band sounded great. I mean, everyone was dancing, and . . ."

"Hey, hey, chill, Albert! I was having a little fun with you!"

The other Orion Stars were laughing, fit to be tied. Albert ducked his head. He knew as well as anyone that Red Dog was the last person in the world to ever feel sorry for himself, but the hangdog, self-pity act had fooled him completely. Red Dog gave Albert's head a rub and went off to the bar with the band. Albert and Daddy sat down at a spool table.

"You liked those Cloud Chasers?"

"Oh yeah, Daddy. They were so cool. The guy? The one with the blue wig? He had the best moves. And he was strong!"

"Yeah, they're something. They were here once before, and now Miss Serena is thinking of having them whenever she roasts a pig."

"But Linden told me that Mocko Jumbies come from Trinidad or someplace! That's really far."

"A lot come from Trinidad, for true. The ones at Emancipation Day, they come from Trinidad. But these Cloud Chasers are homegrown, right over on Big Island. A fast boat and they're here in half an hour."

"They'll be at the next pig roast?"

"I think so."

Albert started to speak, "Daddy, can I . . ."

"We'll see," said Daddy. He stood up and started walking down the beach.

"Come, Albert. Let's go visit with the Cloud Chasers."

Albert followed, hurrying to catch up, stumbling

when the soles of his flip-flops caught in the sand. They were hand-me-downs and too big for him. As they got further from the Jumby Shack, the darkness deepened and the shadows in the dense bush along the beach seemed alive. Even with Daddy right there ahead of him, Albert felt nervous.

Suddenly from out of the dark, a voice said, "Hi, hi, Mon!"

Albert jumped and caught Daddy's hand. The voice seemed to come from a towering Sea Grape tree, and Daddy turned and walked toward it, towing Albert along.

"Hi, hi!" Daddy called, peering up into the leaves.

Seven dark shapes were lined up like birds along a thick branch. Their skinny stick legs reached all the way to the ground. The shapes "hi, hi-ed" back, and everyone began talking at once.

Their talk was ordinary enough—they praised Miss Serena's barbecue and tut-tutted about the tourists dancing tipsily in their flowered shirts. Albert gave his head a shake, marveling. He was on Jumby Bay Beach, in the middle of the night, listening to his father talk with a bunch of guys who were perched in a tree like bananaquit birds, and they were all acting like it was the most natural thing in the world. The calluses on Daddy's bass-playing fingers felt familiar and soothing in the darkness. Maybe it was the most natural thing in the world.

A low voice rumbled, "You're out late, late, Albert. Shouldn't you be home catching up on your Maths?"

Albert just gaped. The Mocko Jumby not only knew

his name, he knew about Maths!

After a moment, his father said, "Albert? Cat got your tongue? Peachy's talking to you, boy!"

Peachy! No wonder the voice sounded familiar! But Peachy on stilts? Peachy sitting in a tree?

Peachy laughed and said, "You look like you just saw a Jumby!"

Albert let go of Daddy's hand, stepped forward, and waved up toward the voice. "Hi, hi, Peachy. You surprised me. I never saw you without a school bus before."

Albert wasn't sure why, but the Cloud Chasers thought that was funny. They joined in with Peachy's "heh-heh-heh," and laughter flowed around Albert like warm honey. Daddy was laughing too, and that always made Albert feel good.

6

Monday Morning

"**M**orning, morning!"

Peachy greeted Albert just like always. Like always, he was wearing his light blue uniform shirt that said "Peachy" on the pocket flap and the faded cap that said "Evinrude Motors" on the front.

Like always, Albert headed for a seat in the middle of the bus. He'd figured out that it was a safe neutral zone between the teeth-sucking disapproval of the church-going girls in the front of the bus and the taunting of the Gatling Creek boys in the back. He sat hunched, his stomach knotted, dreading the day ahead, the week ahead. Everything was just like always, except worse. Much, much worse and he didn't know why.

He had spent Sunday afternoon in his spot on the back deck thinking about Saturday night at the Jumby Shack and about the Mocko Jumbies. They were so cool, and Peachy was the coolest of all. He tried to remember everything they had said about the music they liked and where they performed. He liked that they were regular guys with regular jobs who also were Mocko Jumbies. It was as though they had a secret, mystery life, and he liked being in on the secret.

It wasn't until he went to bed that Monday morning thoughts vaporized his Saturday night thoughts and left him lying rigidly awake and anxious. Monday was the twenty-sixth day of school—he had counted during the night—his twenty-sixth day of pretending everything was fine. There were 153 more days ahead of him. They might as well have been 153 light-years.

He looked at Peachy's straight back and wide shoulders. As he carefully steered the bus down the long, winding descent, he didn't seem like the same person he had been on Saturday night. Albert's own shoulders felt rounded. His mouth was dry, and when he rubbed his hands on his uniform trousers they left moist stains on the fabric. He smiled a pained little grimace. He didn't feel the same either.

He shook his shoulders and lifted them straight like Peachy's. That felt better. He stretched his arms and found himself doing one of the rubber-arm wriggles that the Mocko Jumbies had showed him. That felt even better, so he did a couple more. His arms took on a life of their own. And whack!

"Ow!" His wrist smacked against the metal back of the seat in front of him. Painfully. There was a burst of laughter from behind him, and he slumped back down in his seat. What was wrong with him? He went to all the trouble of sitting where he wouldn't be teased and then went and busted a move that got him laughed at anyway. His shoulders rounded again.

He caught Peachy's eyes watching him in the rear-view mirror. Peachy lifted a hand off the steering wheel and gave him a "thumbs up." His eyes, framed in the mirror, crinkled almost closed from the smile that was splitting the unseen part of his face. Albert tried to smile back, then turned to look out the window. Everything was just like always, only worse. To his horror, the familiar burning began in his throat and behind his eyes. He thought he was done with that! He dug his nails hard into his palms. Can't cry, rather die.

Peachy wheeled the bus into the school driveway and levered the door open. Students shuffled noisily down the aisle and out into the schoolyard.

Silton Stanley tapped Albert on the head as he passed, saying, "Hey, Little Man, you asleep or something?"

Albert stayed in his seat; Peachy's mirror eyes, alert and watchful, stayed on Albert. The silence seemed to deepen as the sun heated the empty bus. Albert stared down at his hands. He could feel the drub of his pulse against his shirt collar, and a pressure almost like a noise was building inside of him. He had to stand, he had to get off the bus, but he couldn't move. The sweat from his palms was staining his trousers. The floor of the school bus was dropping beneath his feet and the walls were moving away. He was falling, but he couldn't lift his arms to save himself. He tried to yell, but his paper-dry mouth was sealed shut and he couldn't even catch his breath. What was happening?

Then Peachy was beside him, gently shaking his shoulder and offering a water bottle. Albert stopped falling; the sides of the bus were no longer moving.

"Hey, hey, Albert. What's going on? Here, take a drink. It's warm, but it's a whole lot cooler than you are right now. You'll be okay. Come on, take a drink, so. You'll be okay. Good. Now breathe. Take a deep breath, Mon, belly breath."

The words were soothing; the water unglued his mouth. He managed one breath, and then another. Peachy sat down next to him, and Albert leaned against the light blue shirt, inhaling the clean-clothes smell. Gradually, the rise and fall of his breath replaced the frantic pounding in his veins. Out of nowhere he began to cry.

If he had been asked about it, Albert might have said that he melted. That's what it felt like, anyway. Like he just melted into an ocean of tears. Peachy might have said something different. But no one asked either of them. And neither of them spoke about it later. Peachy mopped Albert's wet face and every so often said, "You'll be okay, Mon. Just breathe."

After a while, the sobbing slowed and then stopped. Albert lifted his head away from the dark blue splotches that his tears had left on Peachy's shirt and looked around, dazed.

He said, "I'm sorry. I'm sorry. I gotta get to homeroom. I'm sorry."

"Now hold on. Just hold on. I'm pretty sure your home-room must be over by now."

"It's over? I'm sorry. Then I gotta get to history. I'm sorry."

"Albert, y'know, maybe school isn't the best place for you just now. Maybe you better sit this one out."

"But what about . . ."

Peachy fished a mobile phone from his pants pocket and began jabbing at it with his finger.

"But I gotta go . . ."

Peachy gestured him to silence. "I'm calling the school, just a . . . Hello? Miss Ruthie? It's me, Peachy. No, Miss Ruthie, no, my paycheck came on time. . . . No, I don't need an advance. Nothing like that. I'm calling to see if you might want the Cloud Chasers to entertain at that Garden Club Spring Fair of yours."

Albert heard the squeal as Peachy held the little phone away from his ear.

"No, no worries. I'm always happy to oblige the Garden Club. Oh, Miss Ruthie, another thing. There's a kid on my bus here. No, no trouble, it's just he's not feeling too good and . . . Nurse isn't there today? Oh, that's a shame."

Peachy grinned at Albert.

"A real shame. Well, it makes no sense to bring a sick child into the school if she's not there. I suppose I could take him home . . . Okay, if that's what you want, I'm always happy to oblige you, Miz Ruthie. Oh, and you'll take care of the attendance sheet? It's Albert Quashie. Yeah, he's new. Uh-huh, yeah, it's his little brother. Fine family.

Thanks, Miss Ruthie."

Peachy dropped the phone back in his pocket, looking pleased with himself, as though he had just gotten away with something.

"Okay, it's cool. Lucky for you, Nurse is over at Valley Primary on Mondays or you'd be in there right now with one of her nasty thermometers in your mouth."

Albert's mouth puckered for a second at the memory of the bitter rubbing alcohol that Nurse stored her thermometers in.

"Let's get going before Miss Ruthie spies us out the window and decides to drag you in after all. Come on and sit up front."

"But . . ."

Albert couldn't think how to finish his sentence, so he stopped trying and stood up. His legs were so shaky that he had to hold onto the seatbacks. He wondered vaguely how Peachy knew about the nasty-tasting thermometers. He wondered about the falling feeling. He made it to the seat behind Peachy and sat down. At least he'd stopped blubbering like a baby. Then he lay down and was asleep before he knew he was tired.

The next sound Albert heard was waves splashing nearby. Then he heard a big engine rumbling steadily and a smaller engine's high whine. There were voices shouting somewhere, and distant laughter. When he opened his eyes, he recognized that he was on Ferry Dock Beach, near where Daddy worked. He lay still for a minute, taking stock. The rumbling engine was a ferry on its way to Big

Island; the whiney engine was a little fishing boat pulling in heavy with the morning's catch. The wake from the ferry was making the waves splash cheerily against the sand. He was lying on the beach with his cheek on his backpack. What was he doing here?

He heard "Ahright?" and sat bolt upright.

Peachy was sitting with his back against a palm tree trunk munching on a piece of sugarcane. Albert groaned as he remembered what had happened on the school bus. When was that? Judging from the long chewed fibers of Peachy's cane, they must have been on the beach for a while. Peachy rummaged in a wrinkled plastic bag.

He held a fresh piece of cane out to Albert and said, "You know too much of this is no good for your teeth, right?"

"Right," Albert said, reaching for the treat.

Cane was another sweet thing that his mother didn't allow, but he chewed it whenever he could, which wasn't too often since no one on the island grew sugarcane anymore. At the first sweet crunch, he was ravenous.

"This is so good, Peachy. Where did you get it?"

"The Sea Surveyor is in. It's over at the dock unloading concrete and lumber and such from the Leeward Islands. You know those old freighter deckhands—always bring along their farm stuff to sell on the side. I took a walk over while you were asleep and bought it from them. Saw your daddy, too."

"Oh." Albert chewed, but the cane didn't taste quite as good.

"Um, Peachy?"

"Hmmm?"

Silence, then, "Um, Peachy, uh, I'm . . . Albert didn't know where to start.

"That cat got your tongue again?" said Peachy.

"Peachy, I'm in big trouble. I'm going to be suspended. Daddy's going to kill me." Peachy stared seriously down at Albert from under his threadbare hat brim for what felt like a long time, and then his big smile widened across his face.

"You've got one busy, worrying mind between those ears of yours. I bet you see Jumbies behind every tree. You're not in trouble. Miss Ruthie'll fix it with your teachers. And that ferry that just left? Your daddy's piloting, but he's going to make it his last trip of the day. He says for you to wait here and he'll take you home when he finishes the return run. Ahright?"

Albert gnawed at the cane while Peachy's words took root in his mind. He wasn't in trouble. He wasn't in school. And Daddy was coming to get him. He nearly laughed out loud. This was too easy. Maybe it was worth feeling bad for a few minutes in the morning if it meant getting out of school for the rest of the day. But then he shuddered—that falling feeling had been bad. It wasn't worth it, not even to miss a month of school.

Albert looked up at Peachy's dark profile. He wasn't chewing his cane anymore. He was staring out to sea waiting, Albert realized, for him to answer. He was trying to think what to say when it hit him. He owed Peachy a whole lot more than a reply.

"Oh, yeah, Peachy, ahright! Everything's ahright, for true. Sorry. Yeah. Hey, I mean, thanks. Thanks for . . . Thanks. Thanks for . . . um . . . y'know . . . Y'know? I mean what happened . . . in the bus and all . . ."

As Albert ran out of words, his voice got smaller and squeakier until it disappeared completely. He tried again.

"Peachy, you saved my life."

"See, Albert, there you go again with that imagination. Saved your life?" Peachy shook his head and sucked his teeth, but not in a mean way. "You weren't no way, no how dying! Dog tired for true, but not dying. I think maybe you just needed some sleep."

Albert considered that. It was true he hadn't slept much the night before. And after waking from the deep, deep sleep just now, he felt new and bright. Maybe Peachy was right about his worrying mind.

"Well, what you really saved me from was a Maths quiz."

"Hey, Mon, I can fix that, no problem. We leave now, I'll get you back to school quick, quick . . ."

"No, no! No. That's okay. I don't want to put you to any trouble."

Peachy laughed his heh-heh-heh, and Albert giggled like he was in primary school. He couldn't believe it. He was laughing at a Maths quiz! How had that happened? It must be Peachy, he thought.

He studied Peachy's face, but found nothing remarkable in the plain, blunt features or the bald shaved head.

Peachy looked ordinary, but he could do anything. Even walk on stilts. That was cool.

"Peachy, that Mocko Jumby stuff?"

"Uh-huh."

"Where did you get all that—all the tricks and everything?"

Peachy was staring again, past the islands and out to sea. Albert was getting used to Peachy's silences, but this one was really long. Maybe his question was rude. Maybe Mocko Jumby business was secret.

At last Peachy said, "You know what's out there?"

Fishing boats, thought Albert? The Atlantic? What was he talking about?

"Africa," said Peachy. "Africa. Where Mocko Jumbies come from."

Albert felt a shiver in his spine.

"For true?"

"For true. Mocko Jumbies were spirits from long ago that could see into the future. They came to the Caribbean with the people that were brought here in chains from West Africa. My old uncles used to tell us kids stories about how the Mocko Jumbies walked right across the ocean. All the way from Africa. They were following the slave ships that carried our people, trying to protect them. Of course now, well, it's different now. Africa is far away and long ago. Those ancestors are all dead and buried. The uncles don't even tell the stories anymore. But we still have the stiltwalking. We still have the stilts."

Albert looked out toward where he thought Africa

might be. Tickled pink. That's what Mommy always said when she was especially pleased. He felt tickled pink.

After a while, Peachy said, "I know. I know. That's not what you asked me. I learned the tricks and the dancing and all back in Trinidad, too. It's cool. People like it, tourists and everyone, but it's the tradition that's important. The old uncles used to say you have to respect the history. They said every time you get up on stilts, you're a part of history. They told it to me, and now I'm telling it to you, just like I tell it to my kids."

"You have kids?"

"My stiltwalking kids. The ones I teach."

"You teach stiltwalking?"

"A whole bunch of kids from Tattersall High School over on Big Island are learning."

"Kids can stiltwalk?"

"For true. Kids aren't so afraid of heights as grown-ups. Or maybe they're not so afraid of falling. You could try it."

"You'd never get me up on those things. I don't even like stepladders."

Peachy chuckled his deep chuckle and said, "Not for you, eh?"

"No way! Up in the air, so, with nothing to hold onto? Uh-uh. That's dangerous."

"Huh. Up in the air. Nothing to hold onto."

Peachy fell silent and Albert was satisfied that he'd made his point, until Peachy said, "That was you standing on that big boulder by the Jumby Shack, wasn't it? Waving your arms and dancing all around and such?"

"Yeah, that was me," he said, pleased that Peachy remembered him. Then he realized what he was getting at.

"Oh, no. No, no. That's different. I've been climbing boulders since I was little. That's different because . . ."

Because why? He couldn't really say why. He and Linden used to jump into the sea from boulders that were higher than Daddy's stepladder. Why was that different? He bit into his sugarcane.

"Folks sure can be funny about heights . . . ," said Peachy, and let the sentence trail off.

"Me, I don't like heights," said Albert. *Except when I jump off boulders.*

"If you don't like heights, you don't like 'em."

"And anyway, stiltwalking's really hard! I could never do it." *I'd probably fall and break my neck.*

"Y'know, you're right, Albert. Stiltwalking's not for everybody."

"Yeah. It's not for me." *I wish I could stiltwalk.*

"Sometimes I forget stiltwalking isn't important to other people like it is to me. It happens, I think, that most anybody can stiltwalk, but if somebody doesn't want to, well, then, I respect that."

"For true? Anybody?" *Even me?*

"For true."

A loud, dull thud made them turn, and they looked at the coconut sitting innocently still on the sand beside them. It had plummeted silently from the tree above and buried itself in the sand next to Albert's foot.

Peachy said, "Six inches this way and you'd be hurting for true. We better move."

As he stood up, he laughed his heh-heh-heh laugh. "You see that? Just sitting on the beach can be dangerous."

Albert ignored Peachy and he ignored the coconut and sat rock-still, his forehead scrunched, thinking.

Peachy waited for a moment and then said, "Albert? C'mon. They're riper than they look. You don't want to be sitting there when the next one falls."

Abruptly, Albert shot to his feet and grabbed Peachy's arm.

"Even me? Can you even teach me to stiltwalk?"

"Not if you don't want . . ."

Peachy was starting to smile.

"I want to! For true! I really want to!" Albert's voice was a squeaky squawk. "Can you teach me? Please?"

Peachy's smile grew wider. He slipped his arm from Albert's grip and held out his fist for a bump.

"Ahright, Mon, ahright," and then he looked past Albert toward the ferry dock.

"I think I see your daddy coming. Isn't that him?"

7

To Big Island

Albert was nervous. He was sitting under the wide ficus tree, out of the hot sun, with all the other people who were waiting for the ferry. He tipped back and forth on a blue plastic milk crate and scratched the hard-packed ground with a stick. Tuesday and Wednesday and Thursday had slipped by so easily, he almost couldn't believe it. Even making up the Maths quiz hadn't been too awful. He couldn't figure it out. Nothing had changed really. Every day started with a bus ride and ended with a bus ride, and in between classes began and ended like always. Nothing had changed, but somehow everything was different. He'd been looking forward to meeting up with Peachy on Big Island, but that had nothing to do with school. Maybe missing school on Monday had something to do with it. No, that didn't make sense either. What then? He knew just what Chente would say if he were with him.

"Al-bert All-brain, you think too much. One day your head's going to explode." Albert hated it when Chente said that, but just this once, maybe he was right. Maybe he should stop thinking and just be glad that for four whole days school hadn't been horrible.

The ferry came into view, a speck in the distance that grew larger as it approached. Albert stood up, stretched, and then for the heck of it jumped straight up as high as he could to try and touch the rubbery leaves above. He missed, as he expected, and headed to the dock to join the cluster of people waiting for the rusty ferry to swing around and bump against the dock. The engine roared and softened and roared again. Ferry crew and dock crew shouted back and forth. The people getting off bumped into the people pressing forward with their bags and parcels to go aboard.

A policeman wandered onto the dock. Two pickup trucks honked noisily as they reversed onto the dock past the sign that read "Private Vehicles Strictly Prohibited." The policeman shook hands with a couple of deckhands, greeted a couple of friends, and then lit a cigarette and leaned back against the "No Smoking" sign to watch the hustle and bustle that he was meant to control. Albert would have liked to settle back and watch too, but he had to attend to business.

Albert had always taken it for granted that ferryboat captains let other ferryboat captains' families ride for free. When he was with Daddy or Mommy, it was easy enough: A nod from the captain signaled the deckhands to let them walk onboard—no tickets, no problem. By himself, it didn't seem so easy. He peered up to the wheelhouse, where the captain should have been, but all he could see was the glare of the afternoon sun reflecting blindingly off the windows. What if the captain didn't see him? Or what if it was a Big Island captain who didn't know Daddy? He had money for a drink and a phone call, but that wasn't enough even for a one-way child's ticket.

He scooted this way and that, jumping up and down and waving at the wheelhouse. Stepping backward, he stumbled over a shopping cart that a very large lady was pulling toward the boat. He twisted awkwardly to keep from falling and thrust his hands out in case he did. To his horror, his hands landed on the broad bosom of the cart's owner. The soft flesh yielded alarmingly underneath the loose, flowery fabric tent of her dress. He snatched his hands back as though from a fire, and lost his balance completely. He fell hard, landing on his shoulder, taking the cart down with him, the cart full of coconuts.

"Nasty child! You watch where you put those hands!" the big woman shrieked. Faces turned toward her, and she jumped at the chance to tell an audience what she thought of rude kids nowadays, especially Albert. Hot and clumsy with embarrassment, he picked himself up, righted her cart, and tried to gather up the rolling coconuts. The woman ignored his apologies and kept on scolding. He wished he were dead. No, he wished she were dead. No, he wished the whole chuckling audience was dead.

He thanked a man who helped him retrieve coconuts and got away from the braying voice as fast as he could. He'd lost a lot of time. All the cartons had been loaded and passengers were stepping onboard. He looked desperately up at the wheelhouse one last time. To his relief, the window was open and the captain was leaning out of it. It was Captain Pancho, one of Daddy's friends. Albert waved frantically up at him and got a wave back. A deckhand beckoned to him, and he ran onboard.

Albert found a seat by a window and hunched as low as he could while still being able to watch the white water churning up along the side of the boat. His heartbeat slowed down; his anger faded, but not his embarrassment. Captain Pancho had been laughing harder than anyone, and that meant Daddy and everyone would hear all about him and the big lady with the coconuts. He shook his hands, trying to rid them of the lingering sensation of where they had just been. For good measure, he did a few Jumby moves with his shoulders. That felt better.

Albert was used to following Daddy's back as he moved smoothly through the snarl of arriving and departing passengers, freight handlers with their pushcarts, and cartons of everything under the sun stacked haphazardly on the Big Island dock. He tried to slide into the flow the way Daddy did, but plastic shopping bags struck his legs, and babystroller wheels nipped at his heels. He ducked as a man hoisted a case of Red Stripe beer up onto his shoulder, and he stumbled against a carton of broccoli waiting to be loaded onto the outgoing ferry. Through it all, he kept a wary eye out for the big lady. He had managed to avoid her on the ferry; he didn't want to run into her now. Or ever.

He made it through the crowds to the end of the dock and went to look for Peachy's taxi—green, he'd said. The "taxi stand" was a patch of gravel surrounded by a sagging wooden fence and guarded by a faded pink booth at the entrance. A sign—Taxi Dispatcher—dangled from a single remaining nail over the doorway, but there was no one inside. It didn't look like anyone had been inside for a long time. Something about the little multicolored taxi vans parked helter-skelter in the lot made Albert think of Mr. Wheatley's goats in their pen next door, and he giggled. A taxi pulled out next to him, kicking up a cloud of dust that made him sneeze vigorously, but he still heard, "Yo, Albert! Here! Over here, Albert!"

It was Peachy, standing in the open front door of his taxi and waving at Albert over the tops of the other vans. Albert waved back and trotted over. Peachy's taxi was green all right, but a wild, limey green color that he'd never seen before. A heap of lumber—long two-by-fours—was tied to the dented roof rack. Stilts? Stilts!

8

Bucket Practice

Albert had never driven into the hills of Big Island before. When he came with Mommy and Daddy, they did errands in the shops on Main Street or visited Mommy's relatives. School trips never went beyond Big Island History Museum or Big Island Botanical Garden.

The farms they passed were bigger than the ones at home on Little Scrub Island, and there were more goats and cows wandering the hillside pastures. They came to a village that was like a bigger version of his settlement—colorful houses set on a hillside to catch the breeze, churches, a few bars.

Peachy stopped in front of one of the bars, saying he'd be right back. Albert slumped down in the seat. He knew that "be right back" usually meant a long wait. To his surprise, Peachy really was "right back." He handed Albert two Styrofoam cups.

"Hang on to these," he said as he started the engine. "Ahright. Let's get going before that goatwater gets cold.

We're on our way now!'

A beautiful aroma reached Albert's nostrils and his stomach rumbled nearly as loudly as the motor. He loved goatwater stew.

"We're on our way!" he echoed. He held the cups as if they contained liquid gold while the taxi zigzagged down the back side of the mountain to the coast road. They turned onto a smooth concrete drive that rose gently through sloping grounds. Tall Royal Palms, even as teeth, lined the drive and seemed to salute them as they passed. The drive ended in a circle, and above the circle sat a long building with seven high arches across the front. It was as pink as the inside of a conch shell, and Albert thought it looked like a palace.

A sign on the lawn set him straight: Big Island Community College. Where Linden's father taught! Used to teach. Linden had told him about it, but Albert had never pictured anything so grand. Now he really didn't understand why The Professor wanted to leave.

Side by side on a bench at the top of the wide lawn, they tucked into the goatwater. The stew was dark and spicy, just like Granny Quashie made it. Albert slurped the last drop and looked around.

"Where is everybody, Peachy?"

"They'll be here. I thought you might want to start out with nobody watching."

"Oh, yeah. Okay. But isn't this for high school kids?"

"For true."

"Then why are we at the college and not the high

school?"

"I work here, so I get to use the basketball court when it's empty."

"You work here?"

"I work a little bit everywhere, Mon. Quit licking that cup and let's get you up."

Albert expected to help unload the two-by-fours from the roof rack, but Peachy ignored the stilts. Instead, he got the two white plastic buckets from the back of the van and set them upside down on the driveway.

"C'mon over here and step up, Albert."

"Step up?"

Peachy tapped a drum roll on the bottom of the pails and said again, "Step up, Mon."

"On the buckets?"

A longer drum roll was the only answer, so Albert stepped up, one foot on each bucket. The buckets seemed a lot higher when he stood on them than when he stood next to them. He teetered and swung his arms to get his balance. Peachy's hand appeared right where he could grab it, and he held it until he felt steady.

"Ahright?" said Peachy.

"Ahright," said Albert, and let go. He was actually feeling more foolish than ahright. In his mind, he'd been striding on stilts like a Mocko Jumby, but here he was standing all shaky and splay-legged on a couple of old restaurant pails, grabbing Peachy's hand like a baby.

"You start to tip, you just catch my shoulder, ahright?" said Peachy as he bent over Albert's shoes, tying them tighter than they'd ever been before. Then without a word, he began tearing strips of duct tape and taping Albert's feet to the buckets.

Now Albert felt scared as well as foolish. With his feet trapped in webs of silver tape, stepping down was no longer an option, but falling down was a real possibility. The pavement looked really hard. He teetered, and once again Peachy's strong hand met his. He caught it without thinking and steadied himself. This was about as much fun as standing on a ladder cleaning gutters.

"Just forget about the buckets and take a few steps."

Forget about the buckets? Was he kidding? Peachy's furrowed forehead told him that no, he was hardly kidding. Then suddenly Albert didn't care about the buckets. He realized he was looking down at Peachy! He was looking down at someone. At a grown-up! He never looked down at anyone.

Peachy cleared his throat and said, "You stepping some time today, Mon?"

Albert lifted his left foot, bucket and all, and swung it forward. The bucket was wider and heavier than he expected. It clunked against the other bucket, swung wide, and finally landed awkwardly out to his side. He wobbled, but Peachy's hand was right there and he regained his balance.

Right foot. Clunk. This time, the bucket plunked down closer to where he wanted it to be. Left foot. The bucket swung forward and landed a little more softly. Right foot. That was better. Left foot.

After a while, Peachy said, "Why are you staring at

those ugly buckets? Look up. At the palm trees."

Walking without looking down was scary all over again. Each step felt as though he were stepping blindfolded off a cliff. Peachy's hand was damp where Albert grabbed it repeatedly with his own sweaty one. No matter how hard he tried, he couldn't stop himself from looking back down at the buckets when he wobbled, but Peachy was patient.

"Palm trees, Mon. Just look at the palm trees," he reminded him.

Soon Albert could take two steps, then three, without peeking down. He tried using his arms for balance instead of reaching for Peachy's hand.

"Palm trees, Mon, palm trees."

His steps got a little longer. He managed to turn himself around and then walked back toward the taxi, Peachy at his side. He tried stepping a little faster, but Peachy made him slow down. He walked in a circle, and then another. Every new thing was a thrill. He even tried walking backward. Once. He wiped his face with his damp T-shirt and kept walking. He didn't want to stop. The sun dropped behind the mountain and Albert kept walking. He was so intent on his walking that he was startled when a pickup truck beep-beeped as it turned into the college driveway.

"Hold up, Mon," Peachy said. "That's good for today."

Albert stood still while Peachy pulled a utility knife from his pocket and quickly—*snick, snick*—cut the duct tape from his sneakers. As he jumped down from the buckets, his legs turned into jellyfish. He made it to the soft grass before his knees buckled, and he collapsed on the ground. Legs splayed wide, he lay back on his elbows and watched as the pickup pulled alongside the taxi and a waterfall of high school kids poured out of the back.

Peachy bumped fists with the elderly driver, and they began talking and chuckling like long-lost relatives. The boys who'd ridden in the back of the pickup truck began play-fighting and knocking hats off, acting as if it were Friday night and they had the whole weekend ahead of them. Two girls climbed from the truck's cab, laughing as if the showing off was for their benefit. Their laughter encouraged more showing off, which encouraged more laughing. The boys' loose T-shirts fluttered with a careless energy, and the girls' big earrings glinted when they moved. Another car arrived, and more teenagers swarmed out.

Albert watched as the group grew noisier, and he watched as Peachy and his friend talked on. And he watched himself sitting on the grass, alone, apart, outside, as usual, but he didn't feel weird or different. Just weary in his bones, and tickled pink.

9

The Ja-Ja Jumpers

Albert watched Peachy as Peachy surveyed the scene. The sun had set and the sky was quickly growing darker. Kids stood in a circle kicking a soccer ball back and forth, while others listened to a large, tinny-sounding boombox. Then Peachy spoke, his voice rising above the music, soccer shouts, laughter, and talk.

"Ahright, Ja-Ja Jumpers!"

Ja-Ja Jumpers? Peachy had never said that before. A foot halted the soccer ball in midair, and a finger clicked off the music. Voices faded and the kids drifted toward Peachy. Albert had never seen a classroom settle down so quickly. Maybe these kids weren't as cool as they seemed. Maybe they were afraid of Peachy. He couldn't wait to see what would happen next. Peachy grinned his big grin and spoke again.

"Everybody ahright?"

"Yeah, Mon, ahright. We're always ahright! You know that, Mon," replied a tangle of voices, laughing and sassy.

These kids were cool, for true. And they weren't afraid. Bats appeared, sweeping like shadows through the evening. The streetlamps lining the drive started to hum and glow, highlighting teeth and earrings and cheekbones. Albert sat in shadow, comfortably invisible. It was like watching TV in a dark room.

Peachy said, "Where's Sharyn?"

A long time seemed to pass, then a girl said, "She got a D on the Bio midterm."

Albert waited to hear more, but it seemed that getting a D in Biology was the only explanation needed. Peachy wasn't grinning anymore, and no one said anything. It dawned on Albert that, in this unlikely place, grades mattered.

"What about Melvin and Lamont?"

"Their granny's turning eighty today, Peachy. Lamont said she said that if they miss her party, it's the last party they'll ever miss. Melvin has his license now, so they might get here later."

Eyes rested expectantly on Peachy's still unsmiling face. Then his teeth flashed again and he said, "I guess I wouldn't want to vex Granny Hudson on her eightieth birthday either."

Albert heard relief as well as amusement in the bubble of laughter that popped into the evening. Maybe these guys weren't scared of Peachy, but they cared what he thought.

Peachy looked over at him, and for a panicky moment Albert thought he was going to be introduced to these cool, unafraid strangers. If he was thinking of it, Peachy changed his mind because he turned away. Albert breathed again, safely invisible once more.

Peachy and the kids talked a bit more, and then suddenly everyone was in motion. Kids grabbed stilt pairs from where they lay on the ground and headed toward the basketball court alongside the main college building. Two boys ran off toward a metal utility shed and, after some clanking and slamming, the big lights over the basketball court began to hum and glow. A girl took a large clump of keys from Peachy and unlocked a door at the side of the college building.

"Last chance! Don't dance!" she called back to the basketball courts, and there was laughter as a couple of others repeated the rhyme.

It took Albert a minute to figure out that she had unlocked the restrooms, and he grinned as a few kids ran inside to take advantage of the last chance. On the basketball court, kids climbed—clattering and clanging—to the top of the metal bleachers. Albert wasn't sure what to do. Should he just walk right up? Move closer but stay out of sight? Find Peachy?

Out of nowhere, Peachy stepped in front of him, his wide shoulders blocking the lamplight. The sudden move startled Albert, and a scared squeak escaped from his throat. He leaped up and brushed at his shorts to cover his embarrassment. Peachy chuckled and said, "Did I wake you, Mon? Sorry."

"Hey, no, I wasn't asleep! I was just . . ."

He couldn't make out Peachy's face, but he heard heh-heh-heh.

"You ahright?"

"Yeah, I'm cool. A little tired, I guess . . . y'know, after all that on the buckets . . . but I'm cool."

Albert took a sip, warm but still welcome, from the half-full water bottle that Peachy handed him. Did Peachy ever have cold water in full bottles?

"Come on," said Peachy, heading back toward the basketball court, and Albert trotted after him.

The top row of the metal bleachers was filled with kids. They were lined up like birds on a wire, sitting with their backs to the court. They kept leaning forward, straightening up, bending forward again, which somehow made them look even more like pecking birds. As they bobbed up and down, they talked and laughed as though they weren't doing anything unusual. Huh. What was this about?

"Ahright?" said Peachy. At that signal, the movement on the bleachers sped up a bit and the laughter subsided. A boy in the middle of the row suddenly launched himself up and away from the bleachers. Albert gasped, but instead of falling, the boy seemed to hang in midair. His torso glided along behind the bleachers, and the big red number 23 on the back of his basketball jersey fluttered in the wind. When he reached the end of the bleachers and rounded the corner, his legs came into view.

Albert wasn't sure what he expected—no one would wear fancy silk costumes to a practice—but it wasn't this.

Each dark leg was tied to a two-by-four with torn strips of cloth. Yellow foam rubber squeezed out like toothpaste between the tight ties. Skinny ankles disappeared into worn-out basketball sneakers that sat on wooden wedges attached to the two-by-fours.

In a few strides, the boy joined Albert and Peachy on the court. Up close, with the boy's sneakers at his eye level, Albert recognized the cloth strips as Batman sheets, like the ones he used to sleep on. A week ago, the swaying, dancing Jumbies in their silky, fluttering costumes had seemed magical to him. Now he knew better. Knotted sheets and battered wood and worn sneakers and sweaty legs—this was the real deal. He felt a shiver of goosebumps, as though he had just swum into a dim sea cave and seen a light.

"Hi, hi, Peachy," came the voice from high above him.

"Hi, hi, T. J.," answered Peachy. "This is Albert. He's watching tonight."

T. J.'s round, mischievous face seemed to drop from the sky as he leaned down to give Albert a fist bump and said, "Ahright, Mon?"

His smile was friendly, and Albert grinned back and reached his fist up. Before he could say anything, the other Ja-Ja Jumpers gathered around and he was enclosed in a thicket of two-by-fours. He wasn't a part of the conversation that was going on high over his head, so he slipped between the stilts and climbed into the bleachers. If he was going to watch, he might as well get a good seat.

The practice reminded Albert of gym class. A really hard gym class. On stilts. Walking around on the light plastic buckets had worn him out, but every time these guys took a step, they were hoisting a big piece of lumber. And they weren't just walking around.

They started out doing laps of the basketball court with long strides, making tight turns at each end. They practiced standing on one stilt at a time, hopping, hopping, hopping to keep their balance. Their faces were fierce with concentration. They practiced something they called Windshield Wiper, arms overhead, swaying side to side.

Peachy kept up a stream of encouragement, saying, "Ahright! Looking good!" and "Chin high, high—look at the palm trees!" and "Move your arms smooth, so!" but he never said, "Take a break!"

The stiltwalkers wiped their dripping faces. They were breathing hard, but they never stopped moving.

Then Peachy said, "Ahright! You two. You go on up!"

T. J. and a girl named Shirleen began to climb the bleachers. On stilts. When they reached the top bench they walked, faces like stone, along the entire length of it. On stilts. Albert, terrified they would fall, didn't draw a breath until they had clanked safely back down to the basketball court.

Then, half crazed with relief, he leaped to his feet, clapping and yelling, "Ahright! Ahright!" at the top of his lungs. In the quiet following the banging of the stilts on the metal, Albert's voice hung in the air and all eyes turned toward him.

His cheeks flamed—was he going to be "Little Man"

again?—but T. J. laughed in a pleased way and said, "Hey, thanks, Mon!"

T. J. did a deep clownish bow that made him lose his balance. Peachy's heh-heh-heh rose over the laughter of the others as some imitated the bow and the stumble. Albert, relieved all over again, joined in.

Saturday at the Sunshine

Albert stretched his legs. Ow. He rolled over. Ow. His belly muscles hurt like they had the time Headmaster made everyone do sit-ups because no one would say who put the baby goat in the boys' room. He wriggled his fingers. They seemed to be the only things that didn't hurt.

His mother called again. "Albert? Come on, baby. Rise and shine."

He groaned. Across the room, Chente rolled over and mumbled in his sleep. Ashanti probably didn't hear a thing. He sat up and put one foot on the floor. Ow. He put down the other foot. Ow. He stood up and took a few steps. Ow. Ow. Ow. How was he ever going to work at the bakery for four hours?

"Albert, don't you make me late now!"

Albert reached for the shorts he had left on the floor when he got home from Big Island the night before.

"Dress nicely!"

Ow. He slipped off the basketball shorts and flip-flops

and started over. How had he gotten himself into this?

It had taken all week. On Monday, Mommy had said "no!" as soon as she heard about the stiltwalking. Stiltwalking was dangerous. And Albert was too young to be out alone late at night on Big Island. And he was especially too young to be out alone late at night on Big Island running around with high school kids who were probably real troublemakers. And who was this Peachy, anyway? Daddy vouched for Peachy, but he left the decision up to Mommy.

Albert begged and argued and whined. He asked his brothers to back him up, but Chente said he was annoying and even Ashanti told him to stop whining. When he refused to do his chores and threatened to leave home, they laughed at him. Albert had always thought he was pretty good at talking his parents into things, but not this time. Mommy wasn't budging. He settled into an angry sulk. By the time he slammed out the door on Thursday morning, his whole family was very tired of him. If only Linden were here—he'd know what to do. And at least there'd be someone who wasn't tired of him.

As he was getting off the bus on Thursday afternoon, he paused to tell Peachy that he wouldn't be at stiltwalking practice on Friday after all.

"It's because Mommy thinks I'm still a baby, that's why," he answered before Peachy asked.

Peachy looked at him for a long time, then said slowly, "A baby. Huh. Now why do you suppose that is?"

He held Albert's eyes for a moment longer and then

said, "See you in the morning."

Albert hopped off the bus step and headed home, muttering to himself and kicking viciously at stones in the road. He was mad at his whole family, but mostly he hated Mommy. He was in Middle School, and she was treating him like a baby. Even Peachy said . . . Albert stopped walking. What *had* Peachy said?

" . . . *why do you suppose that is?*"

What was he talking about? Was he agreeing with her that Albert was a baby? Now he was mad at Peachy too. He kicked a stone so hard that it hurt his toes and tears started burning in his eyes. He would have liked nothing more than to sit down and let the tears flow, but instead he dug his fingernails into his palms. *Can't cry, rather die.* He didn't want anyone to see him standing by the road crying like a baby.

And that's when it hit him. *Like a baby.* He'd been acting like a baby all week long. Was that what Peachy meant when he asked, ". . . *why do you suppose that is?*" Maybe he figured out that Albert was the reason Mommy hadn't budged. Albert felt pretty foolish, but at the same time he thought maybe it wasn't too late. He convinced Mommy he was too young by acting too young. Maybe he could act grown-up and change her mind. He forgot about his sore foot and ran the rest of the way home, his mind racing even faster. He had to think of a way to do this. He tossed his backpack down and looked around. His neglected chores seemed to be everywhere. He got to work.

He washed the dishes from breakfast. He swept the

deck and he swept the front steps. It was a start, but it was all stuff he should have been doing anyway. He had to do something else, something that would make Mommy forget all the whining, something really grown-up. He paced back and forth, out onto the deck and back inside, his brain on fire. Passing through the kitchen, he caught sight of a yellow Post-It on the wall by the phone. It said "MARISA???" in dark black marker, underlined twice. He stopped and stared at it.

Marisa worked at Mommy's bakery on Saturdays, but she was going off-island for a month to visit family. Her replacement had called Mommy the night before and said she couldn't make it after all. Mommy was worried. Saturday was her busiest day. That was it! *He* would be Marisa's replacement! He knew he could do it. He'd spent plenty of time at the Sunshine, and Marisa's job didn't look hard. All he had to do was convince Mommy. If she let him work, then she would have to admit he was old enough to go to Big Island.

Albert had a cup of tea ready for Mommy when she arrived home. She looked surprised and a little suspicious at first, but when he started talking she sipped slowly and didn't interrupt. In his most serious voice, he made his offer. He didn't whine or beg or sulk, and Mommy listened. It was easier than he had expected. Before she had finished her second cup of tea, Albert had permission to go to Big Island on Friday nights and a job at the Sunshine on Saturday mornings. It had seemed like the perfect solution on Thursday afternoon, but now, on Saturday morning, stiff, sore, and exhausted from the bucket-walking, it felt more like a pact with the devil.

"Okay, okay, I'm coming," said Albert as he hobbled out of the bedroom.

Ellie was already at the Sunshine when they arrived. She squealed and came waddling out from behind the counter, squashing Albert in a monster hug and giving him way too many slobbery kisses.

"Albert, you sweet baby! You came to visit Ellie! You came to work? Momma Quashie, what do you mean putting this baby child to work? Why, it seems like yesterday he was running around in here in a T-shirt with his sweet little bottom right there for the world to kiss. And you're telling me he's going to work? Oh, my, no."

Albert, trapped in those crushing arms, felt himself growing younger and smaller by the second. He stiffened, terrified that Ellie might try to kiss more than his forehead. He freed an arm and gave his belt a tug just to make sure he was still wearing pants. The bell on the door jangled and Ellie looked up to greet Mrs. Stoutt, the first customer of the day. Albert made his escape.

"Gotta get an apron."

He ducked through the swinging door into the sweltering kitchen. Miss Alice, who had been baking at the Sunshine for as long as Albert could remember, straightened up from one of the ovens with a muffin pan clasped in her oven mitts and bent to retrieve another. Mean Miss Alice. She was as small and bony and wrinkled as Ellie was large and round and smooth. In all the years he'd known her, he'd never seen her smile. Her faded blue dress, crisscrossed by apron ties, clung damply to her back. The cords in her thin neck tensed with the effort of lifting, and gray kinks were working free from beneath her headscarf. She seemed tired and old.

He swallowed the lump that had appeared in his throat and said, "Morning, morning, Miss Alice. You want some help with those?"

She jumped, turned, and screeched, "Albert Quashie, what do you mean sneaking up on me like that! Get on out of my kitchen!"

Mean as ever, thought Albert, irritated that he'd bothered feeling sorry for her. He snatched an apron from a hook and darted back through the swinging door. Mrs. Stoutt was laughing at a story Ellie was spinning. He let the flimsy door clack shut behind him, and from the way they both looked up at him, he guessed he knew who the story was about.

"Morning, morning, Mrs. Stoutt," said Albert.

"Hi, hi, Albert. Ellie tells me you're working here now."

"It's nice to have him underfoot again. It's just like when you were little, Albert. Remember the time . . ."

"Albert," Mommy interrupted Ellie, "it's going to get hot, hot in here if you don't roll that awning down before the sun hits. And sweep the front while you're out there."

The bell jangled cheerily as the door shut behind him. Whew. He was safe from the twin terrors of Ellie's kisses and Miss Alice's anger, if only for a few minutes. The awning crank was rusty, and he needed all his strength to move it even a quarter-turn. The sun was hot and soon his sweaty hands were sliding uselessly on the handle. The job was already harder than he expected. What if he couldn't even lower the awning? What if Mommy fired him? He tried using both hands but still managed only a half-turn. He heard the sound of wheels crunching on the gravel and was surprised to see Fast 'n' Furious pull into the parking lot.

"Red Dog! Hi, hi!" he called as Red Dog strolled over for a fist bump.

"Hi, hi, Albert. Working hard?"

"Hardly working," answered Albert, giggling. It was a dumb and not-funny joke that Daddy and his friends said to each other all the time, but no one had ever said it to him before. He had to hide his delight by giving the crank an extra-hard jerk.

When his hands slipped, Red Dog took the handle and said, "See that? Lift until it clicks, then turn. Smooth, so."

Albert tried, and with a few easy turns lowered the faded green and white canvas into place.

"Okay. I get it. Thanks."

He wouldn't be fired after all. He picked up the broom and started sweeping just to make sure.

"How come you're out so early, anyway?" Albert asked.

"You're not the only one working today, Mon. Only way I can get my good-for-nothing crew to work Saturdays is if I bring them a big bag of Choco-Coco Buns. They have any ready?"

"Miss Alice just took a pan out of the oven. I bet they're still warm."

"Cool. Warm is cool."

Red Dog turned and jangled into the bakery. Albert sneezed in the dust cloud he was raising. He felt less sore when he moved, so he swept a little faster. *Working hard?* He smiled. *Hardly working.* He chuckled. By the time Red Dog jangled back out carrying a big bag of Choco-Coco Buns and saying "Don't work too hard," he'd decided that the job wasn't so bad after all.

Back inside, Ellie was singing along with a Christian rock station in her biggest church choir voice as she arranged Mango-Cashew Muffins in a basket. Mommy and Miss Alice could be heard in the kitchen, arguing and banging pans. The warm, sugary smells made Albert's stomach growl. Ellie must have read his mind.

She interrupted herself in mid-hallelujah and said, "Albert, sit down and eat something before we get busy. You want tea?"

"Thanks," mumbled Albert. Ellie set a Styrofoam cup of tea and a paper plate with a Sugar-Sugar Popover in front of him. He was halfway through the popover when the banging and shouting from the kitchen stopped. Mommy came through the swinging door, her face like a thundercloud just before a storm. She shook herself from head to toe like a puppy coming out of the ocean, and the thundercloud disappeared.

She smiled over at Albert and said, "Soon as you're

done eating up all the profits, you can get to work, Albert."

Three more people had come in. Albert stuffed the rest of the popover in his mouth and took his place behind the counter. He pulled on plastic gloves and held a brown paper bag open as he waited for his first customer to decide between a Chocolate-Mango-Peach Muffin and a slice of Banana-Orange-Raisin Bread.

⁂ 11 ⁂

Bad News, Big News

"**M**orning, morning!" said Peachy, like always, a wide smile across his dark face. "How you keeping this morning, Mon?"

"I'm cool. Yeah, I'm cool," said Albert, and he grinned too. Peachy's smile always made him smile.

Albert stuck his fist out for a bump and Peachy bumped him back, laughing. Albert's voice must have been louder than he intended. He felt curious eyes on him as he hesitated instead of going to his usual seat. All day Sunday, he'd been thinking about stilts. Or rather he'd been thinking about buckets. He felt like a baby on the buckets. He desperately wanted to exchange them for stilts. He was sure he could handle the stilts, no problem. He had to talk to Peachy about it right now. He couldn't wait until Friday. Without thinking, he dropped down into the seat right behind the driver.

It was where Anokhi Singh always sat, and she always had the seat to herself. She made a big show of sliding as far away from Albert as possible and pressing herself against the bus window. The girls in the seat behind her sucked their teeth, a chorus of disapproval, which brought muted snickers from the back of the bus.

Albert knew the minute he sat down that he'd made a mistake. If he had just sat by himself in the third row like always, no one would be snickering now. No one would be sucking their teeth at him. By lunchtime, Silton Stanley and his boys would have half the school fist-bumping and saying, "I'm cool, yeah, I'm cool," and the girls would be saying, "Albert and Anokhi, kissy, kissy."

He thought about moving, but he *had* to talk to Peachy. So what if those guys watched him? So what if they laughed? He checked himself out. His stomach wasn't feeling sick. No tears were burning to escape from his eyes. He straightened his shoulders. If he could handle stiltwalking, he could handle the Gatling Creek kids' teasing. He braved a look around, just in case. The boys in the back were laughing, but not at him. They were huddled around something Silton was showing them. He glanced at Anokhi. She was listening to the girls in the seat behind her.

Impulsively, boldly, he said, "Hi, hi, Anokhi," and smiled.

She turned and answered, "Hi, hi, Albert," and then turned away again.

She hadn't returned his smile, but she hadn't sucked her teeth either. He could handle this. He perched at the edge of the seat and rested his forearms on the steel bar between the front seat and the driver's seat.

He leaned forward and said into Peachy's ear, "Peachy, I think maybe I should get real stilts for the next practice."

Peachy answered him by saying, "I heard you were pretty worn out after Friday." Daddy must have been talking.

"No! Me? Worn out? Uh-uh. Not me. I never felt better in my life!"

"For true? No sore muscles?

"Not me! No way."

Albert shifted a little in his seat, and his thigh muscles called him a liar. "Well, maybe a little. My legs might be a little sore."

"A little sore. Heh-heh-heh. Yeah, Mon. That's how it goes. You're feeling muscles you never knew you had. By Friday, you'll be ready to go."

The thought of Friday gave Albert goose flesh—the good kind. At the same time, the thought of the other kids towering above him on their stilts gave him a different feeling. All he could think about was stilts, real stilts.

He tried again. "Hey, Peachy, I mean, the buckets are good for beginners and all, but I think I could learn faster if I had regular stilts. Maybe eight-foot ones."

"All in good time, Mon, all in good time," said Peachy. "A week ago, you wouldn't climb a stepladder to clean gutters. Now you want to jump up on eight-foot stilts? You're a fast learner for true, but that's a little too fast. You stay on those buckets a while longer, ahright?"

Albert was disappointed down to the soles of his sneakers, but he didn't dare nag at Peachy. Instead he said,

"That's cool," and sat back in silence as Peachy steered the rattling bus through the tight turns as the steep, bumpy road dropped to the sea.

When they reached the smooth shore road, the noise subsided and Peachy said, "Albert?"

Albert leaned forward again to listen.

"Your daddy ever take you to the Boxing Day Horse Races?"

"Naw. He takes my brothers. Last year, he told me maybe this year. But he said that the year before too. Mommy always says no."

"Your brothers tell you about it?"

"Yeah, some."

They didn't tell him much. They mostly talked on about their friends and meeting Big Island girls there. Albert always had the feeling that he and Mommy were the only two people in the world who didn't go to the Boxing Day races. Right now, though, he couldn't care less. What did horse racing have to do with stiltwalking?

"Your brothers tell you about the entertainment between races?"

Albert strained even further forward. "No, I guess they forgot that part."

"Yeah, well it's kind of a new thing. See, Boxing Day isn't like the other race days. Folks bring the grannies, bring the babies, make it a family day. So there's a lot of folks who aren't race fans, and they get bored watching horses run around in a circle, so. Now, my brother-in-law's cousin's wife works at the track. She's worked there for years, so she sees things. When she saw people getting restless on Boxing Day, she told her boss he should get some entertainment. Last year, they had a steel band. This year, they want something *more* entertaining. And there's nothing more entertaining than stiltwalkers."

"The Cloud Chasers are going to perform on Boxing Day?"

"The Cloud Chasers? Not those guys!" Peachy laughed. "The only thing those guys do on Boxing Day is digest the dinner they ate on Christmas."

So who, Albert wondered. A troupe from Trinidad? Or maybe . . . "Well, if the Cloud Chasers are digesting, then who's stiltwalking at the track?"

"You can't guess?"

Albert held his breath. It was such a dizzying thought, he almost didn't dare think it. Finally he squeaked, "The Ja-Ja Jumpers?"

Peachy rolled a long heh-heh-heh at the sound. "Ja-Ja Jumpers for true. I got the phone call yesterday. You stay on those buckets for a while yet and you'll be ready to walk on Boxing Day. That is, if your mommy will let you go to the racetrack."

Albert wasn't sure he had heard correctly. Had Peachy really just said that he could perform with the Ja-Ja Jumpers? After just one practice? He sank back into the seat, his head spinning. For a moment, he allowed himself to imagine a racetrack and a crowd of people. He pictured himself bowing as the crowd clapped, as Ashanti and Chente clapped, as the Gatling Creek boys clapped, as everyone he had ever known clapped for him. He ended his daydream with a deep sigh and straightened up in his seat. Something made him look over at Anokhi, but she turned away when he did. Had she been listening?

12

Falling Practice

Peachy drove straight to the college, no stops, and before he knew it, Albert was up on his buckets. Peachy pressed the last strip of duct tape across Albert's sneaker and straightened up. He said, "Okay, Mon. Today you'll be falling."

"Falling? Down? On the ground?" Albert stammered. He didn't like the sound of this.

"Unless you know some way to fall up, it'll have to be down. On the ground," Peachy replied, heh-heh-heh-ing for longer than Albert thought was necessary. He didn't see what was so funny.

"Stiltwalkers can fall, Albert. It's best you learn how to fall right so you don't break any bones."

The ground that Albert was meant to fall onto looked very far away, and his stomach gave a nasty flutter. It was the cleaning-gutters-on-a-ladder feeling. He was disappointed; he thought walking on the buckets had cured him, but the fear seemed to be back.

"Peachy, y' know . . . maybe it would be better if I learned how to *not* fall. Might be safer all around and . . ."

Peachy thought that was funny too. He was chuckling when he said, "Well, that's a fine idea, for true, but it's only a fine idea until you fall. Then it's a bad idea because you're on the ground and maybe something's broken and it's too late to do anything about it."

He moved away from Albert, limbering up his arms and legs. "Watch, now. When you start to go down, don't fight it. Go loose, Peachy style. Tuck your head and your arms and roll. Keep your legs close together and get the buckets out of the way. Peachy style. Loosey-goosey. Nothing broken."

Albert watched as Peachy pitched forward and rolled. He wanted to point out that Peachy was standing on the ground, not on buckets, but Peachy was waiting. He took another look at the grass far below him. There was no getting out of this. He tucked his head, closed his eyes, and dropped. He hit the ground hard, and lay there gasping. The impact had knocked the breath from his lungs.

"Okay. This might take some work," said Peachy as he caught Albert's hands to pull him upright. "Try again."

If felt to Albert as though he'd been falling down for hours when Peachy said, "Five minutes is a good start. Take a break. Water?" He handed over a water bottle, half full as usual, and lukewarm.

Albert took a long drink to calm himself. He felt banged and bruised and mad. He started to sulk, but he caught himself and instead said, "I'm going to walk a little."

He headed off across the broad lawn, his buckets clunk-clunking noisily in the still evening. As his stride lengthened, Albert began to grin. Even though he was sore and beat-up, he loved being up high. Maybe Daddy was wrong. Maybe he didn't have a fear of heights—maybe he had a fear of falling! Fear of falling made more sense, because falling hurt! And maybe Peachy was wrong. Maybe learning to not fall made sense too—if he got to be good at stiltwalking, he would never have to fall again.

Albert tried the Windshield Wiper, swaying his arms side to side as he had seen the Ja-Ja Jumpers do the week before. He kept his buckets moving. It was awkward at first, but it was getting smoother.

"Hey, hey, Albert!" Peachy beckoned with a big scoop of his arm, and Albert clomped slowly toward him. The birds settling in the Royal Palms were starting their bedtime racket. If he stalled long enough, the others would arrive and there wouldn't be time for any more falling.

As he approached, Peachy said, "Give me a hand, Mon. I can't reach to untie this thing."

The rope that held the stilts on the taxi's roof rack had shifted. A crucial knot lay just beyond Peachy's fingers, but from his buckets Albert could lean in and get at it easily. He tugged and twisted until the knot gave way.

"Got it!" he called, pleased with himself. No one had ever before asked him to help when something was out of reach.

"Thanks, Mon. You want to start handing those down to me?"

Albert felt pleased all over again. Two of the tallest high school boys had done this job the Friday before, and Albert knew from watching the way they handled the stilts that it was more of a privilege than a chore.

"No problem," he answered, lifting the first stilt from the rack and lowering it to Peachy. Some of the stilts were really long, so long they threatened to tip him off his buckets when he lifted them. Some had big basketball shoes attached; some had girls' sneakers. Some were painted in colored stripes, and others were decorated with Magic Marker. He recognized T. J.'s by the stray strip of Batman sheet sticking out of a sneaker. And by the letters T and J repeated in blue marker on the wood. Maybe he would write As and Qs on his stilts. If he ever got stilts.

Peachy set the last pair of stilts on the ground, and then he detached a key from the fat bunch hanging from his belt and sent Albert to unlock the restrooms. It was awkward on buckets—he had to bend over double to do it—but he managed. Meanwhile, Peachy turned on the basketball court lights even though, Albert noticed, it wasn't dark yet. A car turned into the drive, and another, and Peachy looked at his watch. He stood alongside the stilts and gathered the kids around him as soon as they arrived. The soccer ball was nowhere in sight, and no radio was playing.

"Ahright?" Peachy called, and voices came back at him.

"Ahright!" "Yeah, ahright." "Ahright, ahright!"

"Everybody's here. Everybody's on time. Even T. J."

That got laughs, and T. J., sheep-faced and smiling, fended off the hands that shoved him and said, "What's up, Peachy? How come we had to be here so early?"

"Well, something's up for true," Peachy said in a low and serious tone, and then stood silently as the Ja-Ja Jumpers sputtered nervous questions.

"What's going on?" "What?" "Something bad?"

Albert felt the same tension for a moment, but he then realized that he knew exactly what was up. In fact, he knew something that the others didn't. He tried not to smile, and he thought he saw Peachy doing the same thing.

Peachy broke the suspense. "Ahright. Here it is. The Ja-Ja Jumpers are gonna perform at the racetrack on Boxing Day!"

There was a fireworks explosion of squeals and laughter that quickly died away.

"Hey, that's only two months away!" "That's a big crowd!" "I'm nervous!" "What if we mess up?"

"Ahright. Ahright," said Peachy. "It's coming up quick, quick, I know, but listen up. You're good stiltwalkers. For true. It's fine you performing for the little kids at the New Testament Church Fun Fair and such, but I think you're ready to strut your stuff for a big audience."

Albert listened as intently as the others as Peachy described what had to be done. Music, costumes, routines, practice, practice, practice. It sounded unimaginably complicated and difficult to him. Only two months away. So much to do.

When Peachy said, "Any questions?" everyone was silent. He broke into a deep, rolling heh-heh-heh.

"Did a Jumby pass by here? Strike you all to stone? Get up on those sticks! We've got work to do!"

That jolted the stiltwalkers into action. They grabbed their stilts and raced to the bleachers.

Albert clomped over to Peachy and said, "Can I use your knife? I have to cut off the tape."

But Peachy didn't hand him the knife. "No, Mon. Tonight you're practicing."

Albert found his voice after a second and said, "But Peachy . . . on buckets? . . . I don't know about . . ."

"You want to just watch from the bleachers while you wait for stilts? Boxing Day's not waiting."

Peachy gave him a friendly whack on the back as he walked away and then turned and said, "Albert, you find some old sneakers and bring them along next week, ah-right? We'll see about some stilts."

13

Sneaker Crisis

Albert headed straight to the closet in the bedroom after practice. He was worried that his feet would no longer squeeze into his old sneakers. The bottom of the closet was cluttered with the stuff that he and Ashanti and Chente had shoved in there whenever Mommy started saying, "Orderly room, orderly mind." He pulled every stray sock and broken flip-flop and toy truck wheel into the middle of the floor, but with no luck. The sneakers were gone. This was bad. He knew he couldn't use the sneakers he was wearing—they were his school shoes, and they had to last. He bulldozed the little heap back into the wardrobe. He wanted to ask Ashanti and Chente if they had seen them, but he fell asleep so quickly and deeply that he never heard them come in.

On the way to Sunshine early the next morning, he asked Mommy about the missing sneakers.

"Those old things? After all the times you wore them to fall in the ocean—you and Linden and your foolishness?

They smelled like low tide. Your daddy took them straight to the dump when you got your new ones."

"Mommy, I've gotta get sneakers! I can't get stilts without sneakers!"

This was the kind of problem that Albert could usually count on Mommy to solve, so with a huge effort he silenced himself—and waited.

After a while she said, "You know, Albert, I'm the only one I can think of that might be close to your size."

Albert glanced down at Mommy's foot as she continued, "You know those sneakers I wear in the garden? They're still in pretty good shape. I take them off before I go swimming—they last longer that way, y'know. And smell better too."

Albert couldn't take his eyes off the trim pink sneaker with its white swirl of decoration poised on the gas pedal. The only difference was that the gardening sneakers had a black swirl. He dreaded what was coming next.

"You go ahead and take them," Mommy said in her kindest, most generous tone. "I won't miss them at all."

Mommy and her hand-me-downs. It was a family joke. Chente called it her other religion. Ashanti said she was allergic to new. Just now, Albert didn't think the joke was funny. He knew she was trying to help, but he was angry all the same. How could she not see how embarrassing it would be for him to wear girl sneakers? *Pink* girl sneakers! His *mother's* pink girl sneakers!

He didn't want to hurt her feelings, any more than he wanted to get her started on "waste not, want not," so he said, "Okay, thanks," and sat quietly beneath the dark cloud that had settled over his bright Saturday morning.

The door jangled and slammed as customers came and went. Talk and laughter filled the little room, and everyone was enjoying themselves. Everyone but Albert. He was thinking about sneakers. He heard a customer say to Ellie, "I listened to the weather just now. There's a tropical storm off the coast of Africa. There's a chance it'll be a hurricane by the time it gets here."

A hurricane! Albert hadn't heard that forecast. He and Linden found great stuff at Hangman Bay Beach after big storms. Maybe he'd be lucky and some sneakers would float in this time. He felt hopeful for half a second, but he realized there was really no chance that two matching sneakers would wash ashore.

He began calculating. He would earn $7.50 for today. If he worked five more Saturdays, he would almost have enough for sneakers, but Marisa was coming back in two Saturdays. It was hopeless. He was mad at himself for spending last week's pay on Ting and candy. He was mad at Marisa for coming back from vacation. He was mad at the customers, though he didn't know why. He was especially mad at Mommy. She had thrown out his sneakers! And tried to make him wear pink girls' sneakers. The hours passed slowly.

At last, Mommy said, "Okay, Little Honey. Ellie's going to close up for me today. Hang up your apron and we'll go."

Little Honey sat in stony silence on the ride home.

That night, Albert tossed in his bed. Sneakers. Money. The next morning, he fidgeted so much during Pastor Robinson's sermon that Mommy clamped a hand on his knee. The faster his mind raced, the slower the service seemed to go. Sneakers. Money. Sneakers. An opening chord from the guitar brought him back to the little church. Albert loved the choir, especially now that a guitarist and a drummer had been added, and he stood to sing.

At the end of the hymn, Pastor Robinson read out the list of people to be prayed for, adding, "And remember that 'The Needy Clothing Distribution' is less than a month away. Look into your hearts! Look into your closets! Those clothes your children have outgrown? Bring 'em in. . . ."

His voice droned on, but Albert wasn't listening. He had an idea. The benediction began at last. He tried to get into the aisle ahead of the rest of the congregation, but Mommy's hand came down firmly on his shoulder and she said sweetly over his head, "Morning, morning, Angelina. Is that hat new? So pretty! Morning, morning, Mr. Rhymer. Yes, it is a blessed day, isn't it?"

Albert surrendered to the pressure on his shoulder. He smiled and nodded at the passing parishioners, even the ones who patted his head and called him sweet. Finally, Mommy released him and walked down the aisle toward the door, but Albert hung back. He was alone in the church. The wide front door framed a square of sunlight in which the ladies gathered, their pastel dresses fluttering and their laughter drifting in the midday breeze. Mommy raised her parasol against the sun, which meant she would be chatting for a while. The coast was clear.

Albert's heart pounded as he moved noiselessly around the altar and through the door of the little storage room at the back of the church. It was crammed with Christmas decorations and choir robes and Sunday school books, but Albert quickly found what he was looking for: the big basket with the hand-lettered sign that read "The Needy Clothing Distribution." If there were sneakers in there, he was determined to distribute them to his own needy self. His stomach felt sicker and sicker as he rummaged through dresses and T-shirts and baby clothes. A voice in his head kept repeating, "You're not The Needy—you're robbing The Needy."

"Albert Quashie?"

Albert gasped and jumped and turned to face Pastor Robinson.

"Hi, hi, Pastor. I was . . ."

He couldn't breathe. Caught stealing from "The Needy Clothing Distribution." And by Pastor Robinson! He was sure to tell Mommy. And if he knew the pastor, he would probably tell Mommy in front of all her friends.

"Albert Quashie, those clothes are for the Needy, now put them back and get on out of here. You kids always looking for T-shirts. How many T-shirts do you want? The good lord provides all the T-shirts you need. For shame! I'll pray for your soul, but I best not find you in "The Needy Clothing Distribution" again. Go on now!"

Albert managed to shove the clothes back in the basket and escaped to the churchyard.

Eyes on the ground, he ran past Mommy, mumbling, "Homework . . . have to . . . bye. . . ."

14

Anokhi to the Rescue

"And if I have to wear girls' sneakers, I'm gonna . . . I'm gonna . . . I'm not gonna. I won't do it. I'll just walk on buckets on Boxing Day."

Once Albert had plopped down behind the driver's seat, he hadn't been able to stop himself. Leaning forward so his lips nearly brushed Peachy's hair, he blurted out the story of the whole miserable weekend. How his old sneakers were gone. How he wouldn't be able to earn enough for a new pair. How he had dreamed he was running barefoot on a burning hot beach and the cool ocean kept moving, receding away from him. Peachy listened in silence, except during the part about Pastor Robinson, when his shoulders shook and little snorting chuckles escaped.

Albert looked around sheepishly. He hadn't meant to say that last part so loudly. Anokhi's dark eyes slid sideways—had she been listening? He leaned back in his seat, embarrassed, but also relieved. The weekend didn't seem so bad now that he'd told Peachy about it.

"Ahright, Albert," said Peachy, and Albert leaned forward again. "I'll say this for you, Mon. You gave it a good shot. But why don't you ask your folks flat-out to help you?"

"No way. Uh-uh. Not this year. Chente starts at the college in the fall. They're saving every penny."

"Oh, yeah, that's right. Your daddy told me he was looking to work extra shifts. Listen to me now, Albert—do you want to walk on Boxing Day?"

"Aw, come on, Peachy. You know I do!"

"You've got brains, right?"

Albert hesitated, thinking about Maths, and said, "Well, maybe, sometimes, a little. Why?"

"I see it like this, Albert. You've got a problem, for true, but you've got brains. You'll figure this out in good time. But you can't be vexing yourself so! Are you hearing me? You take some deep breaths. You can't be thinking sneakers when you're supposed to be thinking Maths. Ahright?"

"Ahright," said Albert, leaning back again.

He wasn't so sure about the deep breaths, but Peachy was right about Maths. If he got a D from Mrs. Scatliffe, he would never see another stiltwalking practice, never mind the Boxing Day races. Reminded, he opened his backpack and pulled out his Maths notebook. He'd spent Sunday afternoon dreading Pastor Robinson's voice calling to Mommy from the front yard instead of finishing his homework.

Anokhi had slid away as though he smelled bad when he first sat down next to her, but now she moved closer.

She was staring at the worksheet lying in his open notebook.

Before he had a chance to speak, she said, "Oooh. That one. Number eight. That vexed me so!"

"Yeah? Me too. All those Xs, and see this . . ."

Albert hesitated but decided to show Anokhi his messy paper. He watched as her finger moved across his eraser-smudged chicken scratches. She murmured to herself as much as to Albert, "Huh. Okay. Hmmmm. Nuh-uh. No way Y is there. Now why would you go and do that? Here, check this out."

She pulled out her own notebook. Albert was surprised to see tidy numbers and letters marching handsomely across her smooth worksheet. Anokhi sat in the back of class with the girls who passed notes and never raised their hands, but he could tell at a glance that she knew what she was doing.

When Peachy pulled the bus to a stop in the school driveway, Albert's homework was still a mess, but number eight was done, and he had redone three other problems. Best of all, he actually understood what parentheses did in an equation. Anokhi had explained it without making him feel bad. Her skinny legs whisked past him and down the bus steps while he was still scrambling to close his backpack. He hurried to catch up and thank her, but then stopped short. She had joined a cluster of girls, and together they moved toward the school door like a single, scary, many-legged girl organism. Albert stayed away.

He passed the office as he did every day on his way

to homeroom, but this time he noticed the Lost and Found box next to the secretary's desk. Maybe there were sneakers in there! It was tempting—he had five minutes before the homeroom bell—but the memory of Pastor Robinson's angry face sent him scurrying guiltily to homeroom. How could he have thought that was a good idea?

Albert had taken Peachy's advice. He had breathed deeply and done his Maths and breathed deeply some more. But by the time the bus pulled up the next morning, he was more vexed than ever. He hadn't figured anything out, and he had a new problem. Overnight, the choice of where to sit in the bus had become another problem. He wanted to sit next to Anokhi to show her his Maths, but if he did that, she might think he liked her. Or, much worse, the other girls might think he liked her. It was bad enough being teased by boys, but girls? He couldn't face that. He lowered his eyes and walked to the third-row seat. Anokhi, he realized when he sat down, had watched him pass.

He knew he had done the wrong thing. Anokhi had helped him with Maths, really helped him, and he never did thank her. And now he walked right by her, not even a "hi, hi." He thought about going forward again to sit next to her, but a ripple of giggles in the front of the bus changed his mind. No way was he moving toward giggling girls.

As he watched, Anokhi ducked her head so that her hair tumbled forward and hid her face. Then she tossed her head back, and the shiny black curtain caught sunlight as it flipped through the air and settled on her shoulders. She reached behind her head and gathered it into a stretchy red hair tie. Albert had never noticed how different Anokhi's hair was from the other girls' brown cornrows and beaded braids. She was different in other ways too, he knew. She was Indian instead of West Indian, and her family lived in Gatling Creek even though they weren't Stanleys. They lived there because Mr. Singh worked at Gatling Creek Boatyard repairing boat engines. Daddy said he must be a real expert; the boatyard had never before hired someone who wasn't born a Stanley or married to one.

As Anokhi finished tightening the hair tie, a girl in the seat behind her whinnied loudly and said, "Pony tail, pony tail. Anokhi's a horse."

More girls whinnied, and the giggling got louder. Anokhi was still smiling, but Albert saw a faint flush rise into her dark cheeks and her eyebrows tug slightly together. What was going on? He had assumed she was friends with the Gatling Creek girls. She was always with them at school, but thinking about it now, he realized that she was always at the edge, hanging on. She really was different. How had he not noticed? He felt he was seeing her for the first time.

Anokhi hid it well, but Albert could tell she was hurt. He was angry at the whinnying girls. He wanted to defend Anokhi, but he was afraid of being teased himself, and then he was ashamed of being afraid. He didn't know what to do. The teasing stopped almost as soon as it began, but for the rest of the trip Albert angrily said to himself all the things he wished he'd had the courage to say to the girls. He stayed in his seat while the others shuffled noisily down the aisle and off the bus. A backpack caught him a glancing blow to the back of the head and startled him into motion. He jumped up, gave Peachy a quick fist bump, and ran to catch up with Anokhi. She was trailing behind the many-legged girl organism.

"Hi, hi, Anokhi," he called, then slowed to a walk next to her.

She looked at him, her face serious and her eyes glistening black.

He was embarrassed to hear himself blurt out, "I did Maths last night."

That was stupid. Of course he did Maths last night.

"Hi, hi, Albert," she answered and smiled.

It wasn't a happy, wide smile, but it told him he had, for once, done the right thing. She stopped and held out a crumpled black plastic bag. He hadn't even noticed she was carrying it.

"Here . . . I thought . . . you can . . ."

"What . . . I don't . . ."

He was confused.

"It's . . . here . . . you can . . ."

She thrust the bag toward him. As they stumbled over each other's sentences, Albert took the bag and peered inside. Sneakers?

"But . . . Anokhi . . . what . . ."

"They're not . . . I mean . . ."

Anokhi ended their stumbling with a quick wave and

ran off. Albert looked in again. Sneakers. And they weren't pink.

At home, Albert dumped the sneakers out of the plastic bag and examined them. They were scuffed and worn and the laces were broken. He tried them on—he would need two pairs of socks. But they were sneakers! And they weren't pink.

He did a shuffly dance around the deck in the loose, unlaced shoes and yelled toward the boats on the horizon, "Thank you, Anokhi!"

15

Tutoring

Albert wasn't sure how it happened, but ever since Anokhi held out the plastic bag with sneakers, she and Albert seemed to have an understanding. It was understood that they felt different from the other kids. It was also understood that they were afraid of the Stanleys and would do just about anything to avoid drawing their attention. And they knew that hearing "Albert and Anokhi, kissy, kissy!" was to be avoided at all costs.

So when Albert sat next to Anokhi on the bus, she made a show of sliding away from him in disgust. Albert barely nodded to her and talked only to Peachy. And when Mrs. Scatliffe told Anokhi to sit with Albert and tutor him during Maths class, Anokhi rolled her eyes and looked vexed. Albert sighed and followed her sulkily toward the corner where Mrs. Scatliffe was pointing.

They sat in silence at the shaky little table—no one whispered in Mrs. Scatliffe's class if they knew what was good for them. Albert watched Anokhi scratching tidily in her notebook while Mrs. Scatliffe screeched her chalk across the blackboard. He looked from the date at the top of his blank page to the blackboard to Anokhi's rapidly filling page until he couldn't stand it any longer. He leaned in toward Anokhi's ear and whispered as quietly as he could, "What's she talking about?"

Anokhi almost laughed—he could see her swallow it behind a smile—and started to whisper an answer. Then she stopped and they both looked up, expecting the worst. Instead, Mrs. Scatliffe gave them a tiny nod and went on talking and screeching her chalk. Anokhi and Albert looked at each other in astonishment. They really could whisper! It was an unheard of privilege. It was immediately understood that they would guard it carefully. They kept their voices low and raised their hands a lot.

Anokhi seemed to enjoy whispering explanations as much as Albert enjoyed hearing them. Thanks to her, the Ys and the Xs and the brackets in the problems began to sort themselves out in his head. In between problems, they whispered about other things: the sneakers (her cousin from Trinidad left them behind), the nastiest Stanley (Silton, they agreed), should flip-flops be allowed in school (yes), should girls be allowed to play cricket (yes). When the bell rang, Anokhi ran off and Albert walked alone to his next class.

One Wednesday morning, Albert was curled into a ball with the sheet pulled over his head. He was waiting for his stomach to clench into a knot—Maths was a double period on Wednesday—but nothing happened. Was it possible he was looking forward to Maths? His eyes snapped open and his feet hit the floor. He headed for the kitchen and caught Mommy around the waist in a big hug.

"Now what's going on with you, Albert Quashie?" she asked sternly, but she hugged him back.

"Nothing's going on with me, Mommy, it's those roosters. How can I get my beauty sleep with that noise? I think we should eat more chicken around here."

Mommy laughed longer than made sense—Albert realized he hadn't made her laugh like that in a long time—and kissed the top of his head.

"Mr. Beauty, I'd be happier chewing those old sneakers you brought home than eating one of those old birds. The dogs won't even chase them. Forget about the roosters and put your uniform on. And fetch your brothers up." He released her and headed happily back to the bedroom. It was his turn. Chente and Ashanti roared as he whacked them with pillows.

Ashanti protected his head with his arms and yelled, "Get away! Go! Are you crazy? I'm asleep!"

"Mommy told me to," said Albert, swinging again.

"Mommy's boy—you do everything she tells you! Get out of here, Mommy's boy!" barked Chente.

"I'm not a mommy's boy!" Albert yelled back.

Mommy's boy. Chente knew how to vex him. He brought the pillow down hard with a mighty thump and ran. Chente jumped out of bed, caught him, and pinned him to the floor. Ashanti piled on. Albert tried to holler, but

Ashanti was tickling him and he couldn't stop laughing.

Daddy looked up from the plate of leftover rice and plantains he was eating for breakfast and watched them for a moment.

He shook his head, but he was smiling when he said, "What's gotten into you, Albert? You've gone and turned back into a pest, for true. It was so nice and peaceful around here for a while."

What had gotten into him? Albert didn't want to think too much about it. The memory of the first weeks of school was fading and he wanted to keep it that way. School wasn't so bad anymore. Maths was making sense. And he had sneakers, which meant he would have stilts. He was having a good week.

The last Maths period of the week was on Friday, and at the end of it, Mrs. Scatliffe's voice froze them in place.

"Anokhi Singh! Albert Quashie! Wait, please. I want to talk to you!"

Albert's mouth turned to cotton. Was the good week turning bad? He fumbled his notebook into his backpack and followed Anokhi to the front of the room. He stumbled and bumped his hip against a desk. Hard. He stopped to rub the spot that hurt and thought about limping in hopes of some sympathy.

By the time he stood alongside her, Anokhi was already beaming a dimple-denting smile at Mrs. Scatliffe. Mrs. Scatliffe was smiling, sort of, back at her. Albert relaxed a bit, but he wasn't ready to join the smiling just yet.

"Albert, I was just saying to Anokhi that I think my experiment is a success."

Experiment? Albert waited warily for her to say more.

"I thought it might work out, and I was right."

A sound came from Mrs. Scatliffe's throat that might have been a laugh. She was so pleased with herself that she seemed to puff up, making Albert think of a hen sitting on a clutch of eggs. She dusted her hands together, which raised a cloud of chalk dust, as always. Up close, he could see that the dust didn't just settle on her dress but on her puffy hair as well. That reminded him of Sunshine Bakery Sugar-Sugar Popovers; and at the thought of Miss Alice shaking confectioners sugar over Mrs. Scatliffe's head, Albert had to bite his lips to keep from laughing. Just in time, Mrs. Scatliffe turned to walk around her desk. Albert coughed noisily, and by the time she fixed her eyes on him again he was stone-faced.

"Albert, I don't know what they were thinking of in primary to send you to First Form with no algebra background, but the tutoring is helping."

She doesn't know I skipped a grade! She must think I'm just stupid, thought Albert, but decided it was probably not the time to tell her.

Ms. Scatliffe went on. "Anokhi, after all these weeks of trying to look ignorant, you're finally participating in class." Anokhi's dimples disappeared. "I'm happy to see the tutoring has helped you too. I want you to keep this arrangement next week. Same seats. No arguments, please. I know a good idea when I have one."

Hall passes in hand, Albert and Anokhi walked out into the empty corridor. Albert's backpack thumped awkwardly against his thigh, and he scurried a few steps to catch up with Anokhi.

She said, "It's funny. She scared me so much at the beginning of the year, and now she seems like, sort of . . . she seems like a . . ."

"Popover?" said Albert.

He knew Anokhi had no idea what he was talking about, but it pleased him that she repeated "popover" and giggled with him the rest of the way to study hall.

16

Baby Stilts

"Albert! Albert! Stop! You're giving me a headache with this nagging, Mon! Just stop now and breathe. Deep breath."

"But, Peachy . . . said Albert.

"Breathe, Albert," interrupted Peachy. "Sit down here and breathe."

Albert plunked down on the overturned bucket that Peachy had placed alongside his own. Spread in front of them were battered pieces of wood, a dented metal tool-box, old plastic bags, and rags. Junk. Nothing but a big pile of junk, thought Albert, frustrated. He took a breath.

Trying to sound as calm as Peachy, he began again, "See Peachy, it's like . . . but his voice cracked, and he sounded more crazy than calm.

Peachy interrupted him again. "Breathe, Albert. Just breathe."

Albert gave up on calm.

"I'm breathing! I'm breathing! I'll breathe, but why do

I have to get up on baby stilts? I might as well stay on buckets. If I'm . . ."

"Just listen to me for a minute here, Albert. Listen up one time. I don't want to keep saying it. It's not safe to go up eight feet. It's foolish is what it is. Four feet is plenty tall enough to start."

"But you said I was getting good!"

"You're getting good, for true, and your balance comes so natural. But I'm not putting you right on eight-foot sticks. One day, Mon, one day. Not today."

Albert could see himself: On Boxing Day, he would be the tiny, cute one and the crowd would point and laugh. He would be on stilts and he would still be Little Man. He picked up one of his black sneakers and tossed it from hand to hand. He opened his mouth and closed it without saying a word. Peachy looked like he was carved from granite. There was nothing Albert could say that would move that boulder.

Albert picked up the second sneaker and clapped the soles gently together. After all that trouble to get them, it was a waste to use them for baby stilts. He had to think of something! Maybe he could make his own stilts. Tall ones. Yeah! He would take the sneakers home and make his own stilts. He would keep practicing on buckets on Friday nights, acting like that was what he really wanted to do all along. At home, he would practice on the stilts. Then just before Boxing Day, he would bring the stilts to practice and show Peachy how good he was. Then Peachy would say how sorry he was and ask Albert to be the star on Boxing Day.

Yeah, that's what he'd do. He'd make his own stilts. He needed wood, he knew that, and screws. Chente might help him with stuff from the lumberyard where he worked on weekends, but it would come with a price. He could end up doing Chente's chores for weeks. And what about tools? Red Dog had plenty of tools—he kept them locked in the special chest in the back of Fast 'n' Furious. But Red Dog once told him that a good carpenter never, ever lends out his tools or his toothbrush to anyone. Albert's racing mind ground to a sharp halt—even if he got lumber and tools, he didn't know how to make stilts!

He was right back where he started, sitting on a bucket next to a human boulder. He slapped the sneakers together harder. He would quit. That was it. He would walk away right now. Peachy would feel so bad that he would come right to the house—no, he would come to school, to Maths class, and in front of everyone to beg Albert to come back. Albert would refuse at first. Then he would say okay, but only if his stilts were as tall as T. J.'s. Then Peachy would say, "Sure thing, Mon, anything, just so you come back." And then he would ask Albert to be the star on Boxing Day.

Peachy's voice startled him. "Now what's going on in that head of yours, Mon?"

Flustered, Albert answered, "What? Nothing. I was just thinking a little."

"Well, maybe it's time to stop thinking a little and start doing a lot. You ready to get to work on these things?"

Albert wasn't ready, but he didn't have a better idea. He knew he wasn't going to quit. He felt a little foolish for thinking it. And he wasn't going to be the star on Boxing Day—that was really foolish. Baby stilts seemed to be the only choice. Peachy pulled a water bottle—warm—from the pocket of his cargo pants and handed it to him.

"Ahright?" he asked.

Albert shrugged, then forced a smile and said, "Ahright."

Peachy began rummaging through the stuff in the pile.

"Ahright. Let's see what we've got. Uh-huh, this will work. Let me see if I charged the battery for this thing."

He took a grease-smudged yellow drill from its plastic case, pulled the trigger, and smiled at the whiny, whirring noise.

"Okay, we're good. Now where's that jar of screws? Got it. We're good. Albert, see if you can find some washers while I look for bolts. Maybe in the bottom of the toolbox."

Albert poked around in the compartments of the toolbox until his hands were grimy with grease and he had a little pile of washers. He wiped his palms on the grass, remembering the first time he and Linden had been allowed to look inside Red Dog's tool compartment. They had stood silently at attention in the bed of the pickup as Red Dog slowly lifted the lid. They moved closer and, barely breathing, looked at the glittering rows of shiny wrenches, hammers, and screwdrivers. All sizes and types of screws, nails, and bolts were in carefully labeled plastic containers. Even the rags were folded in a neat stack. He smiled thinking what Red Dog would have to say about Peachy's toolkeeping habits.

Peachy found a stub of a square carpenter pencil and began sketching on a scrap of wood as he explained what they had to do. He was deadly serious about strong stilts.

"You don't want stiltwalkers falling because of weak stilts," he said.

Albert listened and nodded as Peachy listed the steps, but by the third "and then you. . ." he was lost. He was glad he hadn't tried it at home. Using the buckets as a workbench and Albert as a clamp, Peachy sawed big scraps of wood into smaller, carefully measured pieces. Then they glued the sole of each sneaker to a foot-shaped piece of wood, but Peachy said that wasn't enough. He wanted the sneakers screwed on as well as glued on. He gave Albert a screwdriver and took the electric drill for himself, and they began driving screws from the inside of each sneaker through the sole and into the wood.

"You want supports as strong as you can make 'em," he said.

More little pieces of wood had to be added, glued, and then screwed. Peachy talked about weight distribution and material stress while Albert wrestled with his screwdriver. His shirt was sweaty from the effort, and the screwdriver kept slipping in his wet palm. Peachy, his drill whining sharply, was able to place twelve screws for every one of Albert's, but even so Albert felt pleasantly satisfied while looking at the finished products. Each sneaker sat firmly on its own rough, indestructible platform. He lifted one for a closer look.

"Hey, that's heavy!" he said, surprised.

The buckets were pelican feathers compared to this.

"Heavy for true. And that's just the platform. You wait until we bolt them onto the two-by-fours," said Peachy.

Albert tried to imagine what that would feel like. Maybe baby stilts weren't such a bad idea after all.

Two cars turned into the college drive and Peachy said, "Sorry, Mon. We'll have to wait until next Friday to finish these. You stay on the buckets tonight, ahright?"

"I'm cool," said Albert, trying not to look relieved, and he turned to help Peachy load the makeshift stilt factory into the back of the van.

Peachy held out one of the sneaker platforms and said, "See this long part on the side? When you're ready, you just unbolt there, take off the platform, and bolt it onto a longer two-by-four, no problem."

Albert looked where Peachy was pointing and let the meaning of his words sink in.

"You mean these platforms aren't just for short stilts?"

Peachy nodded.

"You mean these same sneakers could be on short stilts for a while and then maybe after a while they could be moved to tall stilts?"

Another nod, and a small smile.

"Aw, c'mon, Peachy," said Albert. "Why didn't you just tell me all that in the first place?"

He'd gotten upset about nothing.

"Well, I'm telling you now," said Peachy. "It was a little hard getting anything past your attitude before. Fetch that duct tape. Let's get you up on those buckets quick, quick."

✲ 17 ✲

Postcard

"Hey, check it out, Albert—from Linden!" Chente said. "He's so lucky. I want to go to New York!"

Albert left his spot on the back deck and came inside to see what the yelling was about. Chente had stopped at L. S. Bertram and Son Quality Merchandise & Postal Sub-Station on his way home from school. As he tossed his backpack on the floor, he waved a grubby picture postcard at Albert.

"Bertie says tell you sorry. It fell behind the cassava bin."

Albert's heart raced as he took the card. He recognized the Statue of Liberty on the picture side; on the other side there was a stamp he'd never seen before and Linden's big scrawl.

"Dear Albert. We live on the 8th floor. We have an elevator. I can skateboard to school. I write to you so you write to me, O.K? Yours truly. Linden. Here's my address." There was a string of numbers and letters and then

"Brooklyn, New York, USA, 11218."

Albert turned the card over and over, as if he might find more words. Yours truly? Was that all? He wanted more! He wanted to know about Brooklyn and a school you could skateboard to. He wanted to hear Linden's chatter and his cackle laugh. From the creases and smudges, it looked like the card might have been behind the cassava bin for some time. Linden had probably been waiting for Albert to answer.

"Mommy! Mommy!" yelled Chente.

"Hush, you, I'm right here," said Mommy. She came out of her bedroom, where she'd been changing out of her bakery dress and into shorts and her gardening sneakers.

Chente handed her a rumpled white envelope and said, "Bertie says tell you sorry. It fell . . ."

" . . . behind the cassava bin. I heard you tell Albert. That man is a disgrace, running a postal sub-station in that nasty store. Who knows what else is lost in there? Why, praise Jesus, it's from Carmela! Just this morning I was thinking about her and missing her so."

Carmela was Linden's mother—she would have more news. Albert crowded Mommy, looking over her arm, trying to read the tight lines of handwriting on the sheets of notebook paper she was unfolding.

"Mommy, what? Can I read it? Let me see!"

"Albert, give me some peace now."

She moved away from him.

"I'll tell you if there's any news for you . . . Hmmm . . ."

She wandered out the door and headed for her garden

chair, and Albert followed silently, straining to hear what she was muttering as she read.

"... September 16th! Bertie must have had this for ... what ... why, weeks and weeks now. Disgraceful. An elevator! Well. Mm-hmm, I would miss my garden too. Fifth grade? Like fifth level? That must mean they held him back. That smart, smart boy? Tsch."

Mommy dropped into the white plastic chair beneath the ficus tree and put her sneakers up on a red, plastic milk crate.

"Brooklyn Caribbean Festival! Hmm. Excited about Johnny cakes and goat water and guineps? She never made such a fuss about them here. Tsch." Her words trailed off until Albert, barely breathing a few feet behind her chair, could hear only an occasional "mmhmm" or "tsch, tsch" as she sucked her teeth. He felt as though he were standing on a red anthill. After a very long time, Mommy spoke.

"Albert, I know you're there. Come sit." She was like a teacher with eyes in the back of the head, thought Albert. She moved her feet to make room for him to perch on the edge of the milk crate.

"Come on, Mommy, what?"

"Well, she says the groceries in Brooklyn aren't so expensive as she expected, and her neighbors are telling her to buy warm coats right now before it gets cold ..."

"Mommy! Linden! What about Linden!"

"Well, it looks like Linden is repeating a year in school. They call it fifth grade there."

"That's crazy! He was supposed to skip a year like me."

"Well, she says they made him repeat a year because they think our schools are backward. How do they know? Anyway, Carmela and The Professor are vexed. And Linden doesn't like being the tallest in class."

Albert smiled at the thought of Linden being teased for being tall. It sounded so much better than being teased for being short. But then his smile faded. What if the kids were calling Linden dummy for being taller and older? The thought of Linden being mocked made him feel bad.

"Albert?" said Mommy. "You listening?"

"Yeah, sure I am. What else is in there?" he said, not sure anymore if he really wanted to know.

"Here's news you'll like—Carmela found cheap flights that fit with The Professor's schedule and Linden's school holidays, so they'll be home for Christmas."

Linden home for Christmas! Albert leaped from his milk crate and jumped up to slap the ficus leaves overhead. They could go swimming! He hadn't been down to the beach since Linden left. They could take the dinghy out, maybe all the way to Pirate Cove. There was so much he wanted to tell Linden about middle school and working at the bakery. And especially about stiltwalking. How was he going to wait until Christmas? He heard Mommy sucking her teeth and looked to see what was bothering her. She had turned back to the letter.

"I never imagined Carmela would be lonely, but she sounds homesick for true. I'll write her back tonight. No, I won't write. She's been waiting too long as it is. All on account of that Bertie. I'm going to call her. Right after dinner. Uh-huh, I'll call her. My first call to America is going to Carmela."

"Hey, Mommy, can I talk to Linden too?"

"No, I don't think so. It's a dollar a minute to the States, even at night."

"I won't talk long, Mommy. I can pay with my bakery money."

"We'll see. Go on and do your homework and we'll see."

Albert hung up the phone and stared at it. Every word had echoed as though he and Linden were sitting in an empty cistern yelling at each other. A hissing noise in the phone line was so loud that they mostly said, "What? What?" Hearing that echoey voice made him miss Linden more than ever. It was as though he had lost his best friend all over again. He felt empty inside, empty the way the afternoons had felt ever since Linden left. And—he glanced at the kitchen clock—he owed Mommy seven dollars. Mommy looked as miserable as he felt.

Daddy, his arm around her shoulder, said, "That's just what happens. Connections to the States can be bad, for true. You can try again."

"No, no more calls," said Mommy. "I don't want to give my good money to the phone company and hope for a lucky connection. It's like gambling! No more of that. I'll wait for Christmas, have a real visit. And there's letters—stamps don't cost so."

Christmas was so far away. Albert gathered his loose-leaf binder and a pen and went out to the bench on the deck. The stars were out, but he could still make out the line between sky and sea. In the light that fell from the kitchen window onto his open notebook, he began, "Dear Linden . . ."

☀18☀

Baby Stilt Practice

The sound of the gray waves slamming against the hull was deafening as the little ferry churned through the water. The sky was as gray as the water, but it wasn't raining. Not yet, anyway, thought Albert darkly, though he wasn't sure because salt spray had blurred the cabin windows.

No one rode outside when the wind was high, so every seat inside the cabin was taken. Albert was wedged into the center aisle with the other standees. They towered above him like trees, stretching to reach the handrails above. Since Albert couldn't reach the handrails, he was clinging to a seatback and trying to avoid having his face mashed into someone's hot armpit every time the ferry lurched.

A thin, serious man in a crisp, white shirt lost his grip on the handrail and pitched sideways across the laps of two pretty teenage girls, his newspaper escaping in a blizzard around him. There was a burst of laughter that continued as people tried to help the man to his feet, only to lose balance themselves as the ferry bucked.

Albert didn't laugh. He worried. What if the basketball court was wet and slippery? In his mind, the wooden stilts had been gaining weight all week long. He didn't think he would be able to lift them, never mind walk on them. And in the rain? He could picture himself slipping and landing flat on his back in a puddle. Maybe Peachy would cancel practice. That thought cheered him, but not for long. He'd waited so long for this day—he would only be more nervous if he had to wait again.

Albert scanned the sky as they drove in silence to the college. As they turned into the drive, Peachy said, "Ahright, Albert? You're quiet today for true."

"It's going to rain any minute now, Peachy," he answered.

"Nah, Mon. This little thing'll blow itself out soon, soon."

"It looks like rain."

"It's just a blow—you know we always get them this time of year. Are you made of sugar now? A little rain's going to melt you?"

"It's going to rain. I know it," was all Albert could say.

Peachy had drilled holes in the platforms that they made the week before, and he had drilled matching holes in the two-by-fours he had chosen for Albert's stilts. Attaching the supports to the stilts was just a matter of slipping bolts through the holes, slipping lock washers over the bolts, and screwing on wing nuts to hold everything together. It took minutes.

Albert looked up from tightening the last one, and Peachy said in his deepest, most serious voice, "Listen to me now, Albert. Every time, every time, every time you get up on these sticks, you check the wing nuts. You make sure every last one is tight. Count while you do it, one-two-three-four, each stilt, so you don't miss one. Ahright?"

Albert nodded and lifted the stilt to stand it up. The weight of the sneaker platform made it top-heavy and unbalanced. It tipped away from him and started to fall. He lost his balance trying to right it. He felt like he was in a wrestling match, and the stilt was winning. If he couldn't manage one stilt with both hands, how was he going to control two of them using just his legs? His face was hot, his stomach was knotted.

He opened his mouth to speak and, to his embarrassment, his voice cracked as he said, "I think it's going to rain."

Peachy laughed his low, rumbly heh-heh-heh until he caught sight of Albert's face.

He stopped himself and said, "Ahright, Mon? You'll be up on these stilts quick, quick. You won't remember what you were scared of."

"I'm not scared!" said Albert. Squeak.

"Ahright, not scared," said Peachy. "Let's stop talking and get walking."

Peachy swung a pair of stilts smoothly up onto his shoulder. Albert tried to do the same, but his stilts had different ideas. One splayed out to the side; the other dropped behind him. Another wrestling match, and the stilts were winning again. Peachy heh-heh-hehed at first, but then showed Albert how to balance them on his shoulder. That was better. At least he could carry his stilts without feeling like a dunce. Peachy scooped up a bulging, black, plastic trash bag with his free hand and bounded up the bleacher seats—clang, clang, clang. At the top, he swung his legs over and sat down backward the way the Ja-Ja Jumpers did at practice.

Albert shifted his grip on his stilts and slowly climbed after him—clang, step, clang, step, clang, step. At the top, he sat down facing backward too. Peachy showed him how to lift his stilts, lower them to the ground, and lean them against the bleachers.

"Ahright?" asked Peachy.

Albert just nodded and reached for a stilt.

"Hold up now, Albert. What did I say before?"

"The wing nuts? We just did them."

"You check them every time, every time, every time. A stiltwalker always checks wing nuts,"

He sounds like Red Dog, thought Albert, but he did as he was told.

"One-two-three-four," Albert counted.

He pulled the other stilt closer.

"One-two-three-and-four. Okay. They're good."

"Put your foot in," said Peachy. "Make sure your sock is smooth. Ahright. Now pull the laces tight, tight. Tighter. How's it feel?"

"Tight," said Albert, wincing.

"Good. That's good," said Peachy.

Because his stilts were so short, Albert had to lean way over to reach the laces. Peachy's stilts were taller, so his knees were bent up around his ears as he tied his. Peachy finished lacing and began rummaging in the plastic bag. He fished out two slabs of tattered foam rubber and handed one to Albert.

Demonstrating on his own leg with the other, he said, "Fold it over, thick against your shin, so. Now wrap it all the way around your leg. That's good. Hold it there for a minute."

He pulled a frayed, yellow towel from the bag and tore it into strips, handed two to Albert, and said, "Tie here and here," pointing to Albert's ankle and shin.

The foam felt clammy against his bare leg, and the smell of rubber and old sweat rose to his nostrils. It was soft, at least, but he wished he had higher socks.

Peachy pulled longer strips of cloth from the bag—bedsheets, it looked like—and said, "Now press your shin so it squeezes the padding up against the stilt, so. Here." He handed Albert a strip of sheet.

"Start down by your ankle and keep wrapping around. Stilt and leg both. Tight, tight. It's okay if rubber squishes out, just so no wood is rubbing your leg. Keep wrapping. Now pull. Tight, so. Once more around. Tighter!"

As he bent to the wrapping and tying, Albert remembered the first stilt practice and how puzzled he'd been watching the Ja-Ja Jumpers' backs ducking and straightening like pecking birds. Now he was one of those backs.

Was he really going to do what he knew came next? He took a couple of Peachy breaths, but there was nothing he could do about his thumping heart.

"Ahright, looks good. How's it feel?" said Peachy.

Albert lifted his knee and gave a little stomp with his stilt.

"Okay, I guess," he said.

It was heavy. And the ties were really tight. It was as though the stilt was holding his leg prisoner and his leg wanted to escape. Maybe that was how it was supposed to feel. He lifted his knee again and gave another little stomp, and another.

"Ahright. Other leg," Peachy said.

His other leg was in prison too. He timidly stomped with one leg and then the other. He looked down and swallowed hard. The ground looked far away and his stilts looked weak and skinny. His palms were slick with sweat.

The cluster of keys on Peachy's belt brushed against the bench with a metallic sound, and in one smooth move Peachy launched himself and stood swaying in front of Albert, shifting his weight from one stilt to the other.

He reached his hands out and said, "Plant your stilts down together. Good and solid. Now slide forward, so. Yeah, bring your butt right to the edge."

Albert planted the ends of his stilts, but they didn't feel very solid. He slid forward until he was barely on the bench at all. He looked up. Peachy was smiling, but there was something serious in his eyes. Albert felt paralyzed, but his arms somehow raised themselves.

Peachy grabbed his wrists and said, "Ahright?"

Albert wanted to yell, "No!" but his tongue was stuck to the roof of his dry mouth. His stomach lurched and a little scream escaped from his throat as Peachy pulled him up to stand. He thought he was falling and, terrified, tried to flail his arms, but Peachy didn't let go. His feet somehow began to imitate Peachy's step-steps and, somehow, he found his balance. He exhaled a whoosh of relief. He hadn't fallen.

Peachy said, "Looking good, Mon. You're looking good! Don't worry! I've got you. I won't let you go until you're ready," and step-stepped in time to Albert's rhythm.

Then he began to walk backward, tiny steps, still holding Albert's wrists, leading him around the bleachers. When they got onto the basketball court, he released one wrist and they walked side by side. Instead of the hollow clunk of the buckets, Albert heard the soft tap-tap of his stilts on the asphalt as well as Peachy's steady murmur.

"Eyes high, eyes high. That's right. Look at the palms. That's it."

Left. Right. Left. Right. Every step was an effort, but eventually they completed one trip around the court and began a second. Albert's stomach had settled at last and his steps were lengthening into strides. He smiled. What had he been so afraid of? They walked another circle— and another.

Peachy said, "I think you got it, Mon! I'm letting you go. Ahright? Keep your eyes high!"

He released Albert's hand. Albert felt an instant of

panic, but he didn't miss a beat. He kept walking. Peachy shadowed him, his big hand out and ready, but Albert ignored it. He was on his own, walking tall. He felt giddy and light, and he couldn't stop grinning.

Overhead, the sky seemed to be grinning too. The clouds were rapidly scattering to reveal late-afternoon blue. Albert thought he'd never seen anything so beautiful. Birds in the palm trees began their early evening chirping, and he thought he'd never heard anything so beautiful. He had never felt so happy. He wanted to keep walking forever. He wanted to stride across the campus, through fields and yards and over fences to shore into the water and never stop until he crossed the ocean like a Mocko Jumby. He giggled.

After several more circles around the court, Peachy said, "Ahright, ahright. Let's take a break."

Peachy stopped and rested his elbows on the backboard of one of the basketball hoops. Albert stood swaying beside him, holding the rim with one hand and wiping his face with the other. He reached for the bottle Peachy was handing him, and in between gulps of warm water he gasped for air.

"Ahright?" said Peachy.

If he'd had any strength left, Albert would have yelled to the sky above that he had never been better in his life, but instead he grinned at Peachy and said, "Yeah. Ahright, for true."

☀19☀

Practice, Practice, Practice

Albert could tell something was different as soon as he trotted from the ferry into the taxi lot. He had gotten used to a routine on Fridays: Peachy would take his time, sometimes dropping passengers off in the mountains, and eventually they would arrive at the college and wait for the other Ja-Ja Jumpers. But today Peachy wasn't chatting with the other drivers the way he usually did. He was already in his taxi, and there were no other passengers. He started the engine before Albert had his door closed, and he turned left instead of right out of the parking lot. Albert was curious, but a glance at Peachy told him to wait and see. They drove on unfamiliar streets and ended up in front of the Cyril Wheaton Memorial High School. Ja-Ja Jumpers emerged from the shade of a wide ficus tree in the schoolyard and crowded around the van. They jammed in impatiently, noisily, laughing, and complaining in the crush of bodies.

"Shotgun! I called it!" said T. J. as he opened the front door.

He put his fist out for a bump and said, "Hi, hi, Albert. Slide over, Mon."

"Hi, hi, T. J. What's up?" replied Albert as he returned the bump.

"Hold on! Hold on!" said Peachy. "You'll be cracking my axles. Some of you are gonna have to ride with Junior."

Junior Hackett wasn't the only stiltwalker with a driver's license, but he was the only one with an uncle willing to lend him a car. Just then, he pulled up behind Peachy's taxi and gathered up the stragglers.

The overloaded van chugged off and Junior's uncle's sedan, just as overloaded, followed behind. T. J. fiddled with the radio until he found the Big Island station, then cranked it up and sang along. The noise grew louder as voices were raised over the music. Albert was deafened and crushed between Peachy and T. J., but he was sorry when the ride ended.

At the college, no one spent time kicking a soccer ball or fooling around. Everyone, even Peachy, grabbed stilts from the roof rack and headed for the bleachers. They clattered to the top and quickly and skillfully tied their stilts on. Albert grabbed, clattered, and sat, too, but he still, after three weeks, wasn't quick or skillful. Soon he was alone, impatiently tugging at a tangled strip of bedsheet. From behind him, he heard Peachy answering a question.

"Finish early? Just because we're starting early? Uh-uh. No way. Boxing Day'll be here soon, soon. From today, practices start early and run long. Lotta work ahead."

Albert expected groans, but what he heard was

"Boxing Day, yeah!" and "We're stepping it up!" repeated in excited tones. He yanked his last knot tight, checked the wing nuts, and hurriedly pushed himself up from the bleachers. In his haste, he wobbled badly. He reached out, but Peachy's hand wasn't there to steady him. He thought he was falling, but he remembered to lean forward as Peachy had told him. He found his balance and caught his breath. He had messed up by rushing—he wouldn't do that again—but even so the heart-swoop feeling of walking tall was still there.

He joined the gently swaying group and fell into their side-to-side, step-step rhythm. On his stilts, Albert was much smaller than the smallest Ja-Ja Jumper, but he didn't care. He wasn't a bucket-walking beginner anymore. He was a stiltwalker, just like them, and he listened up just like they did as Peachy talked. Peachy started the others on striding warmups up and down the court and took Albert and T. J. aside.

"T. J., you work with Albert, ahright? Go beside the bleachers and show him One-Leg. Take it slow! Three hops to start, then switch legs. Remember when you were learning—body straight, eyes high . . ."

"I'm cool, Peachy," T. J. interrupted. "I remember all that stuff. C'mon, Albert. You'll get this quick, quick."

Peachy started to say something but instead strode over to the boombox on the top of the bleachers and changed the drill so that the Ja-Ja Jumpers alternated running forward and running backward to music. Then they practiced the X Move, crossing one stilt in front of the other, spinning around, and then switching legs.

Albert only caught glimpses of what the others were doing. He was concentrating with all his might not to fall. First T. J. had him bend one knee to lift the stilt off the ground behind him and hop three times.

"Just three times, Mon. Then you rest. Peachy's rules," he explained. "It's so your legs don't get tired and weak so you fall. Okay. Three more."

And so it went. Hop, hop, hop, rest. Albert couldn't lift either stilt very high off the ground, but he was getting better at hopping on one stilt.

During a rest, T. J. said, "Check out this grab."

Albert watched as T. J. bent his knee until his left stilt was sticking straight up in the air behind him. He reached back and grabbed it with his left hand, all the while hopping, hopping on his right stilt. He lowered his stilt to the ground and did the same thing on the other side.

"Wow," said Albert, nervously.

Did T. J. expect him to try the The Grab? He could barely do One-Leg.

As if reading his mind, T. J. said, "Want to try? You're steady enough on One-Leg. Doesn't matter if you can't lift high enough. I can hoist it the rest of the way—all you have to do is grab it and hang on."

"Yeah, sure!" lied Albert.

The Grab had always looked hard to him. Now that he was about to try it, it looked impossible. And indeed it was. He tried as hard as he could, but he couldn't even lift the stilt high enough for T. J. to catch hold. Frustrated, he tried bending forward as he kicked back, exactly what T. J. had said not to do, and had to flail his arms to regain his balance.

T. J. said, "It's cool—catch your breath. This is hard stuff! Give it time. We can . . . oh, here comes Peachy. I'll bet good money he's gonna tell you exactly what he told me. You watch."

What was T. J. talking about? Had Peachy seen that last panicky moment? Would he make Albert get back on the buckets? Kick him out of the Ja-Ja Jumpers?

Peachy said, "How's it going?"

"Not so good," said Albert at the same time that T. J. said, "Real good!"

"You guys must be watching different channels," said Peachy. He heh-heh-hehed for a while before he said to Albert, "Your One-Leg's looking good. Looking good. But you're gonna need more than balance for The Grab. If you want to kick up your stick high enough, you're gonna need some muscle too."

T. J. gave a loud hoot of a laugh. "I knew it! I knew it! Here it comes!"

Peachy ignored him and said, "Best way to get the muscles you need is by running. Running every day. Nothing better than pounding up and down those hills by your settlement. Every day. Start tomorrow, ahright? "

T. J., still cackling, said, "Peachy had me running up and down, up and down Blue Mountain for months. Now it's your turn, Mon!"

He reached gleefully for a fist bump, which Albert returned much less gleefully. Peachy left them and waved everyone off the basketball court and on to the grass.

"There's no smooth, easy-walking basketball court at the racetrack. You got to be ready to walk on anything," he said. The practice started over as if from the beginning, but everything was harder on the sloping lawn. Albert struggled to keep up with the others. He was getting better at taking long strides, but going backward was hard. He was sweating and breathing hard, and he wasn't the only one.

T. J. blotted his forehead with his sleeve and said, "Peachy, Mon, I'm dying. How about a break?"

"No problem. Take a break. You're working hard, for true," answered Peachy.

Scissoring his long legs, T. J. went over to a metal shed at the edge of the lawn and sat down on its tin roof. Kids strode after him, some joining him on the roof, others finding seats on a long branch in a nearby Sea Grape tree. Albert, on the shed roof, lay back and watched the clouds move. Between blinks, the evening star appeared and he smiled. With a sigh, he let his eyes close.

Shirelle, one of the girls in the tree, interrupted the birds' evening singing, saying, "I'm so thirsty! I left my water in my backpack. Letitia, honey, come on. Be nice. Go get it for me."

Letitia laughed and answered, "Uh-uh. I can't move, and anyway I'm not your honey. You go get it, and while you're up there get my water too."

The other three girls on the branch joined in, each

claiming to be faint from thirst and hunger.

"Nobody's eaten since lunch, Peachy."

"Yeah. You fetched us up right from school, remember?"

Peachy was gazing, boulder-like, out at the distant ocean, ignoring the complaints washing against him like waves.

T. J. raised his voice, trying to break into Peachy's thoughts. "Hey, Peachy, how about if Junior drives to buy some food for us? It's dinnertime, Mon!"

Junior jumped at the chance to use his new driver's license, saying, "You give me money and I'm gone. I'll go to Dixie's. It's closest."

"Dixie's fries are gooood!" said T. J., and cries filled the air: "No, not Dixie's! Pirate Hut! The fries are better. Go to the Pirate Hut. No way! Dixie's is the best!"

Since Albert had never had fries from Dixie's or Pirate Hut, he stayed out of it. He thought with satisfaction of the five dollars in bakery earnings that he had stuffed deep into his pocket. Whatever happened, Dixie's or Pirate Hut, he could buy fries, just like everyone else.

Peachy didn't answer—he had pushed himself off the shed roof and stood waving at a car that was careening up the drive. It was painted in haphazard red, black, yellow, and green stripes, and Toots & the Maytals drifted from its sound system. The driver waved out the window to Peachy and then steered sharply off the driveway, veering toward them across the lawn. He braked to a stop near the shed and unfolded his long body out of the driver's seat.

He was stick-thin, and a fountain of dreadlocks sprayed from his head in every direction.

Peachy, laughing and shaking his head at the torn-up grass, said, "Josiah, Mon, I guess I'm going to have to come to work tomorrow after all to patch up your foolishness."

Josiah ignored him and said, "Meals on wheels, Peachy. And free delivery. You get what you pay for. Where's Shirleen? Where's my niece? Hey, girl, are you some kind of bird?"

From her branch, Shirleen called, "Hi, hi, Uncle Josiah. Do you really have food in that wreck? Let me at it. I'm starving! Who's that with you? Miss Ursula! Hi, hi!"

"Ahright?" said Peachy, and everyone except Albert turned to listen. A voice coming from the car had caught his attention. He stared wide-eyed as the passenger-side door creaked slowly open. To his horror, the lady from the ferry dock pulled her huge body to upright.

Albert's cheeks grew hot at the memory of chasing coconuts along the dock, and the feel of the mean lady's squishy chest burned his palms once again. He froze and tried to make himself small and invisible, not something a stiltwalker can easily do, even a short one. Fortunately, the other stiltwalkers were in motion, pushing up from their resting spots and striding toward the car, chattering about meals-on-wheels. Under cover of the activity, Albert made for the Sea Grape tree.

As he passed Shirleen, she said, "Hey, where are you going? The food's this way! Miss Ursula is the best cook!"

"I'm not hungry . . . ," Albert mumbled as he ducked through the leaves and settled on a branch. Miss Ursula. What was she doing here? What if she recognized him? What if she said something? He winced at the sound of her loud bark.

"Josiah, fetch up those pans of chicken and rice and peas from the boot. Set them up on the roof where they can reach, so. Don't forget the Johnny cakes—they're on the back seat."

"You just relax yourself now, Miss Ursula. I'm on it," said Josiah.

The stiltwalkers crowded around the car, and when Josiah pulled the aluminum foil from the pans, a happy murmur rose. The peppery smell of spices and coconut milk and chicken reached Albert's nostrils, and his stomach growled savagely as the others heaped their paper plates.

"Peachy, you didn't tell me I'd be feeding wild animals," Miss Ursula said. "I never saw such eating! Don't these children get fed at home?"

Peachy, his mouth full, couldn't answer, and Miss Ursula talked on.

"Children don't eat right nowadays, and it's the fault of the parents. They let them run around all hours. . . ." Shirleen and another girl returned to the branch, their plates bending from the weight of the food. Albert groaned and looked away. What was wrong with him? One minute he was striding around like a Mocko Jumby and the next he was hiding on a tree branch like a lizard. Hiding . . .

from what?

Albert looked over at Miss Ursula standing by the utility shed, still telling Peachy about kids today. He shook his head and looked again. Was that what he was afraid of? A noisy, cranky old lady?

He pushed himself to stand and said, "Maybe I'm hungry after all," and walked toward the car.

Josiah, who had been sitting cross-legged on the bonnet of the car, slid to his feet as Albert approached and began filling a plate for him.

"You just made it, Mon. Food's almost gone."

Albert thanked him, then walked to Miss Ursula.

He took a deep breath and said, "Thank you, Miss Ursula. This looks good."

He forced himself to wait for a reply. She looked up at him, and he forced himself to meet her gaze.

She blinked, then looked back at Peachy saying, "Huh. Imagine that. A child with manners."

Moments later, from where he sat eating in the tree, Albert heard the clatter of aluminum pans being stowed in Josiah's car and the sound of the engine starting. With a wave and some frantic honking, the little car zoomed away across the grass. As suddenly as she had arrived, Miss Ursula was gone.

20

Bad News

Albert woke up confused. He was sure it was Sunday, but it didn't seem like Sunday. For one thing, Mommy wasn't singing along with the Christian station that she always listened to before church. He found her and Daddy sitting solemn-faced at the table.

"Morning, morning," he said as he shuffled toward the sink for a glass of water, but neither one answered.

After a moment, Daddy said, "Albert, come. Sit."

He sat. He looked from one to the other. Something was up. Why didn't they say something? He used Ashanti's old joke to break the silence.

"Whatever it was, I didn't do it."

Daddy gave a small chuckle, but then looked serious again and said, "Naw, nothing like that. You're cool. It's something else. Peachy took a fall at the Jumby Shack last night. He's in hospital, but he'll be okay."

"What? I don't get it. What happened?"

Peachy always said stiltwalkers could fall, but he never

said anything about hospitals. Wasn't that what falling practice was for?

"I don't know for sure. I didn't see it. All I know is he fell. He was lucky—Big Alton had his go-fast boat tied right there on the dock, so they got him to Big Island quick, quick. He's going to be fine, just fine. He's got a hard head."

"He hit his head? That's bad! Did he crack his skull? Did you talk to the hospital?"

Albert was on his feet now, anxious to know more.

Mommy pulled him toward her lap and said, "Settle yourself, Albert. There's no answer at the hospital. You know how the phones can be. But he'll be fine."

"Head like a coconut, for true," said Daddy. "He'll be fine. Don't vex yourself."

Albert pulled away from Mommy. "If he's so fine, why is he in the hospital?"

"That's what they do, I guess," Mommy said. "Red Dog went over with him last night. He told your daddy he'd call if there was any news. So we wait. We wait."

"But . . ."

"Albert . . ."

Albert knew better than to nag when Daddy used that voice. He left the room in silence. Outside on his bench, he stared numbly at the horizon. He was sure his parents knew more than they were telling him. Something was going on, and it was probably bad.

He kept picturing how wild the Devil Wheel routine was when the Cloud Chasers did it at the end of their show.

Maybe someone held on to Peachy's stilt for too long. He pictured Peachy crashing to the concrete. He imagined him unconscious and bleeding and paralyzed for life. He imagined Big Alton's boat racing over the dark water to Big Island. He imagined himself at Peachy's funeral, and with that he jumped up and shook himself like a wet puppy. He had to stop thinking. In the bedroom, he pulled on sneakers and shorts.

At the front door, he called back, "I'm running."

His mother said, "Don't be long. You'll have to shower before church."

Albert broke into a fast, pounding run on the rough road that wound down toward Gatling Creek Bay. It took all his attention to avoid tripping, and he was glad of that.

Later, in church, Mommy reached for Albert's hand when Pastor Robinson said, "Let us bow our heads together now to pray for Peachy Lettsome. He's a friend to folks in our congregation and he's in Big Island Hospital. Let us pray for his speedy recovery, in Jesus' name. Amen."

Two big tears plopped on his lap as Albert bowed his head and prayed for Peachy. Peachy Lettsome. He hadn't known his last name before.

He left Mommy behind in the churchyard and ran all the way home, through the house, and onto the back deck, calling, "Daddy? Daddy? Did he call?"

"It's okay, Albert," said Daddy, pulling himself up from the king chair. "I just talked to Red Dog. Peachy's gonna be fine. His mobile phone's not working, but Red Rat gave me a number that rings on his floor at the hospital. Think we should try it?"

Albert laughed with relief and shouldered into Daddy like a rugby player, pushing him inside toward the telephone. "Yeah, we should. Right now."

He shifted from foot to foot while Daddy dialed—and dialed again. At last someone answered, and he asked for information about a patient named Albert Lettsome. Albert stopped fidgeting. Peachy's name was Albert? He didn't know that. He was tickled pink that he and Peachy were both Albert. He wondered why everyone called him Peachy instead. Maybe he was teased when he was a kid the way Chente teased him. Maybe he should change his name too. What would he change it to?

Daddy's voice, raised, broke into his thoughts. "It's L-E-T-T-S-O-M-E. Albert. A-L-B . . . Albert Lettsome. How is he? No, I'm just a friend. You only talk to family? Well, can I speak to the doctor then? No? Well, can I speak to Peach . . . Mr. Lettsome? I'll wait, sure, I'll wait."

To Albert he said, "Might take a while. She has to go fetch him from his room."

Albert tried not to fidget as they waited.

At last Daddy said, "Peachy! Hi, hi, Mon! Yeah, it's me. I can hardly hear you. What's going on? All Red Dog said was you're alive. A concussion? Oh. . . .Oh. . . .Uh-huh. . . . Yeah. . . . Mm-hmm. . . . Two or three days? Well, sounds like you need the rest, for true. But hey, hold up. Albert's vexing me here. Can you talk to him quick, quick, before he tears my arm off?"

Daddy covered the mouthpiece and said, "Just say hi,

hi and let the man go back to bed."

Albert took the receiver. "Hi, hi, Peachy. Are you really okay?"

"I'm cool, I'm cool."

Albert was shocked at the weak voice. Peachy didn't sound cool at all.

The question that he meant to ask disappeared from his mind, and instead he said, "I never knew your name was Albert."

A faint heh-heh-heh rolled out in response, and Albert felt the knot in his stomach loosen. He exhaled a long breath. Peachy was cool. He'd be okay.

Then the weak voice was back saying, "That was a good laugh, Mon. Made my head feel better, for true."

Albert felt better too, hearing the laugh, but he still had to ask. "Peachy, was it Devil Wheel?"

"What? No, no. Nothing so fine as that. It was just a foolish accident. There's nothing to tell."

Albert couldn't stop himself. "But what happened? What happened?"

"Ahright. Ahright. I'll tell you. You know those plates they have at the Jumby Shack? The plastic ones for the barbecue? Well, someone must have dropped one on the concrete, y'know, where we dance. I never even saw it, but when my stilt hit it, whoooop, it shot out from under me and I went flying. Next thing, I'm on my back."

A stupid plastic plate, thought Albert. No wonder he didn't want to talk about it—it was kind of embarrassing.

He said, "Peachy? Are you there?"

"Yeah, I'm here. I was just thinking it's a good thing I didn't land on a tourist! Heh-heh-heh. . . .Uh-oh. The nurse is coming and she looks vexed. I better go."

Albert hung up, chuckling at the idea of Peachy squashing a tourist. The fall was bad, but Peachy was all right. The stupid plate was embarrassing, but Peachy had laughed at it. And at least it wasn't the Devil Wheel. He didn't feel as worried as he had. Then he smacked his forehead. He had forgotten to ask about Boxing Day. And Friday practice.

On Monday morning, a stranger opened the school bus door, but Albert sat in the seat behind him anyway. The driver—Terrence, turned out to be his name—had told the kids that Peachy had an accident and the bus was noisy with rumors. Anokhi began questioning Albert right away. Her lips got tight as he explained that the accident was a stiltwalking fall, that a concussion was keeping Peachy in hospital, and that he would be fine. She shook her head and blurted out,

"Walking on stilts is asking for trouble. Only a fool would do that!"

Albert was dumbfounded. Why did she say that? She looked too serious to be teasing. He didn't have time to think about it, though.

Girls had been leaning in to listen to him from behind and from across the aisle, and one of them interrupted, "Never mind who's a fool, Anokhi! Albert, is that true? What you said about Peachy? How do you know, anyway?"

"Did you see it?" asked another.

When Albert turned to answer the question, he discovered that the girls weren't the only ones listening. Silton Stanley was at the front of a pack of shoving boys who jammed the bus aisle as they moved forward to listen.

"See what happen?" Silton asked. "The accident? Who saw it? Little Man?"

The babble of voices rose as the girls that had half-heard Albert's explanation offered half-true answers to the questions that the boys were firing. Terrence began to yell. Because he turned the steering wheel as well as his head with each holler, the bus swerved back and forth across the road. Kids screamed and jostled until it jerked to a halt, and Terrence leaped from his seat.

"You fool kids! You trying to make me crash this bus? Stop all this carrying on. Sit down and stay sat down!"

No one said a word, not even Silton, and the boys began shuffling backward. A hand gripped Albert's arm, pulled him to stand, and towed him along.

Silton's grip stayed tight, and he hissed over his shoulder at Albert, "Come on! Come on!"

As Terrence, muttering loudly, put the bus in motion once again, Albert plunked down in the back row with Silton. He rubbed his sore arm and tried not to look frightened at being in enemy territory. His backpack was still next to Anokhi, whose face, turned briefly toward him, looked a mile away. Questions pelted at him from all sides.

"Where was the crash?"

"Was Peachy driving?"

"Was there a lot of blood? Did you see it?"

Albert was flustered by the attention. He waited, shoulders hunched, for the teasing to begin, but it didn't.

Instead, Silton shoved the nearest questioner and said, "Shut up! He can't talk if you don't shut up!"

Albert glanced at the faces leaning in toward him. Were they waiting for him to say something foolish? He wished desperately that he was someplace, anyplace, else, but oddly enough, he was also excited to be sitting with the Gatling Creek boys. He wanted to impress them. If only Peachy had been in a flaming car crash—they'd like hearing about that. He no sooner had the thought than he felt ashamed at being so disloyal to Peachy.

He cleared his throat and nervously began telling them the same story he had told Anokhi. His audience quickly grew bored with concussions and hospitals, but they didn't tease him or push him away. Instead they crowded closer. It turned out that none of them knew that Peachy was a Mocko Jumby, and they didn't know much about stiltwalking either. They fired questions at him and listened to every word he said. He began to relax. He told them about Africa and Mocko Jumby tradition and Peachy's Cloud Chasers, but he didn't say anything about himself and the Ja-Ja Jumpers. Much as he wanted to show off, something held him back.

At school, he retrieved his backpack and walked slowly into the building. It had been exciting to be with the older boys, but also confusing. Just because they liked him today didn't mean they'd like him tomorrow. What if he'd said something that could be used against him later? Silton could turn against him for no reason at all. He shrugged. He would never figure out Silton, so there was no point in trying. But what about Anokhi? Had she called him a fool? Why was she upset? He would talk to her in Maths—she would tell him what was going on.

At home that afternoon, Albert forced himself to change out of his uniform and into shorts. During Maths, Anokhi had only talked about Maths. He felt more confused than ever. On the bus ride home, he'd sat alone, head down, in his old third-row seat. Nothing made sense. Instead of leaping over the front steps to start his run, he walked down them one by one, wondering why he was bothering. Boxing Day probably wasn't going to happen anyway. Maybe stiltwalking was over. His eyes prickled, but he brushed away tears before they could form and ran faster. The pounding of his sneakers would never muffle his thoughts, but it was better than sitting still and thinking them.

Usually he ran to where the road turned into Gatling Creek Settlement and then ran back home, but today he kept running downhill and then turned onto the side road that led to a cluster of little houses. He knew Anokhi lived in one of them, but he didn't know which one. Two little boys were playing in the yard of a pink and yellow house. They had Anokhi's shiny black hair, and their skin was the same color as hers. This had to be it.

He stepped through the pink and yellow gate and said,

"Hi, hi. Is Anokhi home?"

They stopped playing and stared. For a moment, Albert thought he had guessed wrong. Then the younger one let his cricket ball roll from his fingers, hopped onto the porch, and called Anokhi's name through the long strings of beads that filled the doorway. The bigger boy lowered his cricket bat to the ground and kept staring at Albert. Albert picked up the ball that had landed near his foot and tossed it from hand to hand as he waited. When Anokhi pushed through the door and saw Albert, she hesitated for a moment and then sat down on the top porch step. In shorts and a T-shirt, hugging her knees to her chin, she looked like a stranger to him.

Albert didn't feel welcome to sit next to her, but he took a step closer and said, "Hi, hi! I was just out running and I . . ."

He was uncomfortably aware that he was wearing the old ripped T-shirt he'd slept in, and that it was clinging to his skinny, sweaty torso. Anokhi's silence wasn't helping.

"Did you get stuck on the Maths again? You don't have your book with you," she said.

"Uh, well, no. I mean I didn't start it yet. I was just out running and I . . ."

He stopped again. He wanted to run away.

Instead he crossed his arms, took a deep breath, and said, "Look, I mean, you know I'm a stiltwalker, right?"

She nodded.

"So what you said before, on the bus, you think I'm a fool?"

Anokhi lowered her forehead to her knees for a moment before answering. "No, no. I'm sorry. I don't know why I said that. No, yes I do. When you told me about Peachy falling, it made me remember something. When I was in third level, before we moved here, my teacher was a stiltwalker. He was always talking about it, and once he even walked for us after school. He was so cool. But one day he didn't come to school, and everybody said it was because he fell. Some kids said he broke every bone. He never came back, and this mean lady taught us for the rest of the year. I missed him every single day. I guess hearing about Peachy and remembering my teacher just got me all upset."

"So you don't think I'm a fool for true?" asked Albert, surprised that it mattered so much what she answered.

"No. No, for true, I don't. I was being foolish. I mean, I'm from Trinidad! We invented stiltwalking! I think it's cool, but I still think it's a little dangerous."

Albert grinned and uncrossed his arms.

He felt as though he'd received a gift of some kind, and he wanted to thank Anokhi, but instead he said, "Okay. I guess I better go start the Maths."

Anokhi stood up and said, "Yeah, me too. I'll see you on the bus. I hope Peachy comes back soon. I hate Terrence."

"Yeah, me too. See you tomorrow."

Albert waved and then slipped through the gate and out of the yard. Then he turned back and said, "Hey, Anokhi, y'know, stiltwalking was invented in Africa, not

Trinidad!"

He could still hear her laughing and calling him a liar as he broke into a trot for the uphill run home.

21

More Practice

Albert jogged anxiously to the Big Island taxi lot that Friday afternoon. He looked around for the lime-green van with its stack of stilts on the roof, but it was nowhere in sight. He didn't know what he was doing here. There probably wasn't any practice. He went over to the taxi drivers who were waiting for fares and asked if they'd seen Peachy.

"He's in hospital, Mon. I don't think he's coming back."

Albert was frightened all over again until another driver said, "Naw, Mon. He went back to Trinidad—a funeral. Someone died, maybe his aunt. Or maybe a wedding."

"I heard he got a good job, government job. No more taxi for him!"

"No, Mon, it was Cockroach got that job, not Peachy. Peachy's still driving, same, same like us. Haven't seen him, though."

Albert relaxed. They were just spinning rumors. They

didn't know any more than he did. He decided not to give up on Peachy. He would wait until the very last ferry back to Little Scrub if he had to. He thanked the drivers and found a shady spot where he could keep an eye on the taxi lot and the ferries. He didn't have to wait long. Junior pulled up in his uncle's car with a load of Ja-Ja Jumpers squashed inside with him.

Over his shoulder to the back seat, Junior said, "Ha! See—I told you. I knew he'd be here."

To Albert he said, "Hi, hi, Albert. Get in!"

The rumors started flying immediately, though they weren't as farfetched as the ones he'd heard at the taxi stand. Junior said his father had seen Peachy in the hospital on Tuesday. No one had seen him or spoken to him since then, though. So, like Albert, the stiltwalkers had decided that the only way to find out if there was a practice was to go to practice.

When they got to the college, they found some Ja-Ja Jumpers there already staring at a pile of stilts lying like pickup sticks on the ground. Peachy's boombox was there too, and his bag of rags and foam rubber, but there was no sign of Peachy or his taxi. Everyone was talking.

"Why would Peachy just leave the stilts here?"

"Maybe it wasn't him who did it."

"Well, who else?"

"Maybe Peachy's dead and somebody stole his taxi and that's who left the stilts."

"That's plain foolish, Mon. Don't talk like that!"

"Just take it easy. Peachy's okay."

"How do you know? Junior's daddy saw him and his head was all dripping blood and . . ."

"I never said that! All I said was . . ."

"I called him ten times—no answer!"

"I called too, and my neighbor lady said . . ."

"Who cares what your neighbor lady said? I think . . ."

"You can't answer the phone in hospital! Don't you know that?"

"He's not in hospital anymore!"

"Well, what do we do now?"

Albert's gaze rested on the pile of stilts. Listening to the arguments and rumors was making his stomach clench. If only someone would stop standing around and do something. He spotted his own stilts in the pile and, without thinking, he tugged them free, hoisted them onto his shoulder, and headed for the basketball court. The conversation stopped behind him. He realized that the others were probably staring, but he kept walking.

T. J. broke the silence. "Who cares who brought the stupid stilts? They're here, so I'm gonna get up on 'em. Wait up, Albert!"

There was a pause, and then everyone was in motion. The bleachers shook and clanged as the other stiltwalkers joined Albert and T. J. at the top.

T. J. said, "Y'know, we'd probably still be arguing if you didn't make your move."

Albert bent to his stilt ties to hide a proud smile. He wasn't sure how he did it, but he had started something. That was cool.

By the time everyone's stilts were tied on and the Jumpers were milling around on the basketball court, it didn't seem so cool anymore. T. J. was trading fake punches with guys at one end of the court. There was bickering about what to do, and Albert felt anxious all over again. When he noticed Shirleen and Junior off by themselves whispering intently, he felt a little better. Shirleen, in her bright lipstick and big earrings, was the biggest, bossiest girl he'd ever seen. She was as good-humored as she was loud, so no one ever seemed to resent her demands. Junior was quiet and undemanding, but Albert had noticed that he often managed to get his way. They were the oldest and, hands-down, the best stiltwalkers. If anyone could figure this out, they could. As he watched, they seemed to come to an agreement. Shirleen stepped to the middle of the court and hollered for everyone to listen. She and Junior had come up with a plan.

"Y'know how Peachy's been saying we might have to drop Devil Wheel? Well, we were thinking if we work just on that tonight, get it right, he'll have to let us keep it in."

Albert was the only one who didn't jump happily at the idea. He thought Devil Wheel looked scarily difficult when he saw the Cloud Chasers do it at the Jumby Shack. Now that the Ja-Ja Jumpers were trying to learn it, he knew that it was impossible. At least for him. The Grab was the most important move in Devil Wheel, and he still couldn't do it. Despite running every day and doing extra practice on Fridays, he couldn't swing his stilt high enough behind him for anyone to grab it. And on top of that, he was afraid of what would happen if he ever could swing it high enough. What if he lost his balance? What if the person holding his stilt didn't let go in time? All the falling practice in the world wouldn't save him from a fall like that. Just thinking about himself in the Devil Wheel made him nervous.

During practices, Albert stayed in the Devil Wheel routine until they got to The Grab. Then he would step aside and watch as the others formed the Wheel. He was pretty sure that on Boxing Day, Peachy would leave him out entirely. He'd been secretly hoping that Peachy would drop the whole routine instead of dropping him out of the Devil Wheel.

The Ja-Ja Jumpers moved into position and someone started to chant, "Devil Wheel! Devil Wheel!"

Albert felt like a traitor for hoping it would be dropped and joined in with the chant. Suddenly, Shirleen stopped dead and looked at Junior. He stared blankly back at her and then smacked his forehead with his palm. They both cracked up. Albert figured out as quickly as the others what was funny, and he laughed just as loudly. They had forgotten about the boombox. It lay on its side on the court, far below the reach of anyone wearing stilts.

Junior said, "At least Peachy didn't see us being so foolish!"

There was another burst of laughter. The tension was gone. Junior went to take off his stilts and retrieve the boombox. By the time he had his stilts tied on again, Shirleen was already leading the Ja-Ja Jumpers through Devil Wheel. As usual, they lagged behind the music and the song ended long before they finished the routine. They looked discouraged, but Shirleen acted as though she had planned it that way all along.

"That was great, you guys! Really great! "

Even Junior looked unconvinced at that, but Shirleen wasn't giving up.

"Take a little break and we'll do it again."

Albert had stepped away as he always did, when The Grab started, and watched the rest of the Devil Wheel. It made him think of the whirling, spinning hubcaps on Fast 'n' Furious. Suddenly, like a jellyfish sting in the brain, he had an idea. He wanted to scream it out to Shirleen, but she and Junior were huddled together again, and they didn't look happy. Did he dare?

He walked over and said timidly, "Shirleen?"

"Just a minute," she said, without looking at him.

He tried again, louder. "Shirleen, I noticed something in Devil Wheel."

She and Junior both turned.

"Noticed what?" she said.

"At the end, making the Wheel, everybody gets behind."

She and Junior exchanged impatient looks.

She said, "Well, yeah, no kidding. That's why we're practicing it."

She started to turn her back on him, but Albert blurted, "Wait! Sorry. I mean . . . what I mean . . . is what if you tried two Devil Wheels? One inside the other? And when the Wheels move, they could go in opposite ways, y'know? Like those fancy hubcaps that spin in two directions?

Smaller circles, smaller steps, so nobody gets behind. I bet it would look really cool too."

Junior and Shirleen began whispering again. Albert waited, step-stepping uncertainly, his eyes on his stilt tips. They were probably mad at him. Why should they listen to him? He couldn't even do The Grab! Should he say he was sorry?

But the next minute, Shirleen's big voice was calling everyone together. It took her a couple of tries to explain it, but once they got it, the Ja-Ja Jumpers wanted to try it. It wasn't easy to get the two Wheels moving without stiltwalkers crashing into each other, but after three tries they managed to do it without hurting anyone. They took a break, and Shirleen strode over to where Albert was leaning against the bleachers.

"You saved it, Albert. Your idea worked for true. Peachy has to let us do Devil Wheel now."

Albert reached up to bump her extended fist. He liked the praise, but his idea guaranteed that he would sit out for the entire Devil Wheel on Boxing Day. He didn't like that at all.

Shirleen said, "Listen, you're not the only one with ideas around here. Wanna hear mine? It's about you."

Albert nodded. "Okay."

"We're going to do it again, but this time, when we start The Grab, you don't walk away. You go right into the middle."

Albert stared at her. Go into the middle and do what? *What was she talking about?*

Junior joined them and said, "Just try it, Mon. Can't hurt. It's better than standing around looking all sad. You can bust some moves, try stuff. You'll be like . . . like . . . the axle of the Devil Wheel. I mean Wheels."

Albert wanted to answer, but what came out was ". . . but but but . . ."

Shirleen leaned over and almost in a whisper said, "Albert? You okay?"

He was better than okay. His heart was heavy and full of gratitude. For the first time, he felt like a real Ja-Ja Jumper. Tears threatened to spill onto his cheeks, but he managed to nod and smile.

Shirleen pulled him into a hug and, using her big voice again, said, "Aw, doesn't Albert have the cutest smile? Doesn't he?"

Her friends giggled, and she kissed him on the top of the head so they would giggle more. Albert made a weak attempt to shrug out of her arms and everyone laughed harder. He was embarrassed, but no one was mocking him. They were laughing the way the Orion Stars laughed at Red Dog. He'd never felt embarrassed and happy at the same time before.

Shirleen got everyone into place, and they began again. When The Grab started, Albert slipped between dancers and into the center of the circle. He began a side-to-side step, careful to stay right in the middle, careful to stay with the music. When the two Wheels were complete and the Ja-Ja Jumpers were hopping in place, Albert stood still. At a signal from Shirleen, the dancers moved forward, making the Wheels turn, and Albert started to dance. He added Windshield Wiper to his side steps, swinging his arms in wide half circles.

Shirleen called to him, "Try the X Move! Go on! Try it."

He nodded, crossed his stilts, and spun himself around, and then he did it twice more. Then he began running in a circle in the opposite direction of the inside Wheel. It was dizzying, everyone in motion, two Wheels spinning in two different directions, Albert racing. He came back to the center in time to do a final X Move just as the song ended.

Shirleen screamed as though she'd won the lottery. "Perfect! That was perfect!"

The others joined in. "We got it now!"

"Oh, yeah!"

"The best! We're the best!"

Junior said, "Nice move, Albert, running the circle at the end, so!"

Sweaty and proud, the Jumpers noisily congratulated themselves. Shirleen and Junior made sure Albert got the credit he deserved for his idea, and he returned more high-fives and fist bumps than he could count.

Suddenly over the noise, someone shouted, "It's Peachy! Hey, hey, look! Peachy's here!"

Albert turned so quickly that he nearly fell off his stilts. It was indeed Peachy. He was standing outside the court, fingers hooked into the chain link fence, watching them. A large white bandage above his left ear stood out against his dark skin and Albert stared worriedly at it.

Peachy gave his widest smile, though, and Albert couldn't help but grin back. Peachy released the fence and walked toward the gate, trying to answer the questions that the stiltwalkers who shadowed him inside the fence were firing at him.

"Peachy, what happened? Was there a lot of blood?"

"Is your skull cracked? Does it hurt?"

"Where have you been? I tried calling you."

"Who brought the stilts?"

The mystery quickly dissolved. Peachy had dropped the stilts off on his way to the clinic for his last appointment. His skull wasn't cracked, not even a little. It was a little concussion, no big deal. He was fine—the doctor just now told him he'd be back on stilts in plenty of time for Boxing Day.

"And you guys, working hard so! I call out 'hi, hi,' nobody even turns my way you're working so hard. I'm proud of you, for true. That Devil Wheel? That Devil Wheel never looked so good. It looks Boxing Day good."

22

A Bad Week

"**A**nybody? Nobody?" Mrs. Scatliffe tapped her chalk against the long equation that marched menacingly across the blackboard as she surveyed the room, looking for a raised hand.

"How about you, Mr. Quashie? You think you can solve this one? Come up here."

She seemed angry as she lowered her chin and glared at Albert from beneath her colliding eyebrows, but she always seemed angry, and he'd gotten used to it. He got to his feet, thinking it wasn't so long ago that he would have tried to drop through the floor if she had called on him like that. Of course, she never used to call on him at all. As she handed him the chalk, he thought he saw something like a smile at the corners of her mouth.

The Xs and Ys and parentheses within parentheses within parentheses seemed to go on forever. Without meaning to, he moved ever so slightly in the side-to-side motion that he used to steady himself on stilts. As he looked at the equation, the parts began organizing in his head. He loved it when that happened. He could see what she was up to. The equation looked scary because it was so long, but it was really just a lot of small equations strung together. Nothing new. He could do this. He took a breath and began scratching away at the blackboard, but Mrs. Scatliffe stopped him.

"Speak, Albert. Say what you're doing!"

What? Stand there in front of the whole class and explain how he solved it? Wasn't that *her* job? He hated her.

He glanced around the room. Silton, fortunately, was busy playing with a pencil. Anokhi smiled encouragingly. He remembered the first time she explained a Maths problem to him, how she had done it without making him feel dumb. Maybe he could do that. Yeah. He could do that.

He faced the equation again, breathing, rocking, thinking, and then turned to the class and blurted, "It's a trick!"

Heads swiveled to look at him and then, expectantly, at Mrs. Scatliffe. Anokhi looked worried. Uh-oh. That came out ruder than he intended. It probably shouldn't have come out at all. He didn't dare look at Mrs. Scatliffe and, not knowing what else to do, he took a deep, Peachy breath and rushed on. He marked with his chalk as he explained how stuff on one side of the equals sign canceled out stuff on the other side, until all that was left was a simple, straightforward, and familiar equation that had been hidden there all along.

When he finished, he was pleased to hear a few voices

say, "Ooooohhhh, I get it."

He set the chalk in the tray and moved to sit down, but Mrs. Scatliffe said, "You see a trick here, Mr. Quashie?"

He stared with deep interest at a crack in the floor tile. Now she was mad for true. Was she going to send him to Headmaster for being rude?

He coughed and said, "No, ma'am. I mean yes, but not exactly . . . , " and stammered to a halt.

"Well, now, did you solve the equation?"

This was safer. He answered more strongly, "Yes, ma'am!" But he kept his eyes down waiting to see what came next.

"Well now, how can a trick be a trick if the trick didn't trick you?"

What was she talking about? "Um . . . I don't know?"

Mrs. Scatliffe ignored him. She was talking to the rest of the class about how they were all mathematicians, how an equation can never trick a good mathematician, but Albert wasn't listening. He was trying to figure out how to escape back to his seat.

" . . . and that's because Albert is a good mathematician."

His head snapped up. He couldn't believe his ears. He didn't hate Ms. Scatliffe anymore.

" . . . but he's not the only one. There are good mathematicians in this room who don't know yet how good they are. It takes a little work. It takes a little patience. Sometimes it takes a little help from other people, from tutors. Ms. Singh has tutored Mr. Quashie, and now he knows that he is a good mathematician. Now it's his turn."

The next thing he knew, Albert was back in his seat at the little table watching Anokhi gather up her books. He didn't look up when Silton slammed his backpack down and slumped into the chair that Anokhi had just left. Did Mrs. Scatliffe really expect him to tutor Silton? He heard a chair scrape and turned to see Anokhi slide into the seat next to Silton's cousin Barton. And how was Anokhi supposed to tutor Barton? Even Silton called him Bean-Brain Barton. Mrs. Scatliffe rustled around in her big, flowered carrybag until she found the folder she was looking for.

She took out mimeographed sheets and began handing them out, saying, "You'll do the first equation right now and we'll go over it together. The rest are for homework. Silton and Barton, you may talk to your tutors as long as you keep your voices low. Any questions?"

Silton rolled his eyes. Albert realized that he probably didn't have to worry anymore about failing Maths, but now he had a new worry. Silton was obviously unhappy with this new arrangement, and Albert had a pretty good idea who he was going to take it out on. He hated Mrs. Scatliffe.

That afternoon, Albert collapsed on the porch step after his run. He was exhausted and gasping for breath, but he had to smile. He'd been so mad at Mrs. Scatliffe that he hadn't even noticed he was tired, and he'd run faster and farther than ever before. At least hating her was good for something! He caught his breath and went inside.

Chente was on the couch clicking the TV remote and saying, "Nothing. Nope. Nope. Nothing. Postcard from

Linden. Nope. There's never anything on in the afternoon."

"Wait—postcard? Where is it? What did he say?"

Albert found the postcard by the sink, a picture of someone dressed up like the Statue of Liberty standing on a box with a crowd of people around. "Dear Albert, The Aunts for Christmas. Home on Boxing Day. See you soon!!! Sincerely, Linden."

For weeks, Albert had been imagining telling Linden about stiltwalking and taking him to the racetrack on Boxing Day so he could see for himself. He imagined how impressed Linden would be, imagined himself saying, "It's not so hard, Mon." But no matter how he read it, the postcard put an end to his imagining. "The Aunts" lived on Big Island. Linden would probably be leaving Big Island on Boxing Day just as Albert was arriving.

"What's all the sighing? Did your crazy little buddy write you some bad news?" said Chente.

He left the couch and stopped to knuckle Albert's head on his way to the refrigerator.

"He's not little," said Albert irritably as he swatted Chente's hand away.

Friday was the last practice before Boxing Day, but the stilts lay on the ground untouched. The Ja-Ja Jumpers circled restlessly. They should have been up and practicing, but Peachy had said costumes first, then stilts.

The problem was that the costumes hadn't arrived. Albert wasn't sure what was happening; he just knew that Miss Ursula was in charge of costumes for some reason, and for some reason she hadn't brought them the week before as planned. Waiting was making everyone edgy. What if the costumes didn't come? What if they didn't fit? What if they were ugly?

"She'll be here soon, soon," said Peachy. "And I told you nine times already: one size fits all. They'll fit for true. If they're ugly, well, just close your eyes. Now everybody chill, ahright?"

At last Josiah's little multi-colored sedan tooted up the drive, and it was swarmed before he had braked to a stop.

"Hi, hi, Miss Ursula! Hi, hi, Josiah. Where are they? In the back? Let's see!"

Albert hung back. He wasn't frightened of Miss Ursula anymore, but he wasn't about to run up and demand a costume from her.

Josiah bounced from the car like a skinny jack-in-the-box, saying, "Back, now. Get back! We've got 'em. Just take it easy."

Miss Ursula slowly heaved her roundness out of the car, sputtering loudly, "No manners. No patience. That's what's wrong. . ."

Josiah opened the trunk and hoisted out an over-stuffed black trash bag. It tipped as he set it down, and colorful silky fabric spilled out. The wind billowed the cloth, threatening to sweep it away.

Peachy moved quickly between the costumes and their would-be wearers and said, "Shirleen, Letitia, come give Josiah a hand."

To the rest of them, he said, "Ahright? Here's the deal.

Miss Ursula made trousers and a vest for everybody. They go on right over your clothes. Just make sure you wear a white T-shirt on Boxing Day. A new one. Or a clean one anyway. You got that?"

"But Peachy, what if one size doesn't fit my size?"

"Yeah, me and Arturo aren't the same size for true."

"One size is one size, Mon. As long as your T-shirt is white, you'll look like a calypso star."

Miss Ursula sorted through the tumble of costumes, still grumbling about manners. It took a while, but eventually the confusion died down and everyone ended up with a costume. Albert's was dazzling. The striped vest had every color in the world, and streamers of ribbon hung down from it. He held the trousers up. They dropped to the ground and beyond in tiers of bright blue, gold, and red. He loved it. He could picture how it would look when he danced.

But when he slipped on his one-size vest, it fell off his shoulders. And he had to clutch his one-size pants with two hands to keep them from falling down. And then there was the problem of walking on human-length legs while wearing stilt-length trousers. Everyone else had figured out how to roll up the mile-long pantlegs. They were walking around as if they'd been wearing the costumes all their lives, but the yards and yards of slippery fabric seemed determined to trip him up. It was worse than wearing hand-me-down school uniforms.

Peachy called out "Ahright?" and the costumed, excited Ja-Ja Jumpers gathered around.

Feeling as though he were in a sack race, Albert hurried to catch up. He hadn't gone two steps before his legs got tangled in the cloth and he fell full-length on the grass.

He heard Peachy again say, "Ahright?"

As he kicked to free himself, he muttered under his breath, "No, I'm not ahright. Do I look like I'm ahright? What . . ."

"You, boy! Stop that! You're going to rip it!" Miss Ursula bellowed, almost in his ear.

"Sorry, sorry. I tripped," he said, still struggling, but more carefully, to stand up. "I just . . ."

"Hold still!" she barked. He froze on one knee, propped on one hand. He was very uncomfortable, but he wouldn't have moved if a scorpion walked across his face.

"You're a Quashie boy, aren't you?" she bellowed. "Lift that arm! Hold still! Let me get at that vest! Stop squirming! Your daddy's a ferry captain, isn't he?"

"Yes, ma'am."

Did she ever talk in a regular voice?

"Now let's get the trousers off quick, quick. Watch what you're doing!"

Albert tried to cooperate as she bent her big body over him, but everything he did was wrong. She tugged at the twisted fabric, breathing hard.

"Lift your foot! No, the other one! I hope your daddy isn't one of those captains that bang the boat hard into the dock, so. Shake up passengers. Careful! Your sneaker's caught! Hold still!"

By the time Miss Ursula was done with him, everyone

else was in the bleachers tying on their stilts. He watched as Miss Ursula stumped away to join Josiah, his costume under her arm.

Cries of "Thank you, Miss Ursula! They're beautiful! We love you! Thank you!" trailed after the little car as it drove off, taking Miss Ursula and Albert's beautiful one-size costume with it. Albert stood and stared. Miss Ursula hadn't said anything about bringing the costume back. Now what?

High-pitched squeals made Albert look around. The stiltwalkers were on the basketball court striding giddily and laughing noisily. Waterfalls of jewel-colored fabric fluttered around their stilts. They looked like magical wizards from a primary school storybook. No wonder they were so excited. Albert sighed.

He watched for a moment and then looked down at his basketball shorts. He sighed again. He'd been doing a lot of sighing that week. Then he gave himself a shake. Enough! Maybe he couldn't do anything about Linden missing the Boxing Day races, and maybe he couldn't do anything about Mrs. Scatliffe making him tutor Silton, but he better do something about this costume, and fast!

He ran toward the basketball court, calling, "Yo, yo, Peachy! I got a problem, Mon!"

23

A Gift

"You can't? Why not?" said Albert.

He realized he was still holding out Anokhi's present, and he pulled his hand back, embarrassed. He was sweating from his run, and the moisture had ruined the paper he had carefully wrapped around the little box. Anokhi's eyes were on the ground, her shoulders were hunched, her hair hid her face. She looked as uncomfortable as Albert felt.

She cleared her throat and said, "We don't celebrate Christmas."

Albert said, "Oh, Seventh Day Adventists. Ellie that works at Mommy's bakery is Seventh Day too, but she loves getting presents anyway. I guess your family's more strict, huh?"

Anokhi laughed at that. Albert didn't know what was funny, but it was better than having her look as though she were going to cry.

"We're not Seventh Day. We're Hindu."

Albert knew Hindu was a religion, but beyond that

his mind sputtered. Confused, he asked, "Because you're from Trinidad?"

"Of course not. Not everyone from Trinidad is Hindu. Peachy isn't. And not everybody here is Christian, either, y'know."

Anokhi's shoulders had straightened, and she was looking at Albert again. Albert wasn't embarrassed anymore, just curious.

"For true?" he asked.

"For true. There's three families living over by Swanson Bay. And my uncle's family and some others on Big Island. Remember when I was absent a while ago? I wasn't really sick. We were on Big Island for Diwali."

"For what?"

"Diwali. It's my favorite holiday. The Festival of Lights. You visit everyone and everyone has little oil lamps and candles everywhere. And there's candy and presents, new clothes. It's great. It really is."

Albert thought for a moment and held out the gift again and said, "Merry Diwali?"

Anokhi hesitated, then took the box with a shy smile. As she unwrapped it, the soggy paper disintegrated and stuck to her fingers, making them both laugh. She took off the lid and lifted out a delicate chain. A small pendant— two curved pieces of silver, crossed in the middle—caught the afternoon light.

She said, "Oh! It's silver!"

"See, I got it because it looks almost like an X, like X in an equation. Get it? It's a Maths necklace! Y'know, because you're good at Maths."

Albert had been idling in a Big Island souvenir shop while waiting for the ferry home when he saw it. A Maths necklace for Anokhi had seemed like a brilliant idea then, but now he wasn't so sure. The pendant didn't really look that much like an X, and the thin bracelets that always jingled on Anokhi's wrists, he realized, were made of gold, not silver. Now it seemed more like a stupid, embarrassing idea.

"I've never seen a Maths necklace before. It's pretty!"

Anokhi lifted her hair so that Albert could help her put the necklace on. He rubbed his palms on his shorts, but the little clasp kept slipping in his sweaty fingers.

At last, he got the hook through the silver eye.

"There. Got it. Whew."

Anokhi dropped her hair and, fingering the X, turned to smile at him. "Thanks, Albert. I really like it. "

He beamed with relief, and there was a pleasantly odd silent moment between them.

Then Albert thought to say, "How come you said you were sick for the lights thing? If you miss school for church, you don't get in trouble, y'know."

She hesitated before she answered slowly, "No, I know. I mean, I don't know. It's not like it's a secret or anything, but if I said it was for Diwali, then everyone would say, 'What's that?' and 'What's Hindu?' and then I'd feel all different and weird."

Different and weird.

Albert said, "Yeah. Yeah. I hear you."

Anokhi smiled and shrugged and Albert smiled and shrugged back at her, and there was another little silence.

Albert said, "Well, I better finish running."

"How come you run so much anyway?" she asked. "Do you really like it?"

Albert started to answer but stopped himself. Just the day before, Chente had entertained Ashanti by imitating the pained expression on Albert's face as he panted back into the house. The two of them laughed even harder when Albert insisted that he really liked running.

He didn't see the point in repeating such an obvious lie to Anokhi, so he said, "Naw. I hate it. I guess it's getting a little easier, but I still hate it."

"Why do you keep doing it?"

Now he wished he had just said he liked it.

"Well, see, there's this thing on Boxing Day that's sort of like . . . well . . . ."

"Yeah, the stiltwalking thing. I know all about it."

"You do? Who told you?"

"Nobody. I hear stuff when you and Peachy are talking."

Albert wasn't surprised. He knew she listened, but he didn't know how much she heard.

"How come you never talk about it anyway? Is it supposed to be some kind of secret?" she asked, watching his face intently.

Albert didn't know how to answer. He didn't think he was keeping it a secret. Mommy and Daddy knew, of course, and Ashanti and Chente, but they had all stopped asking him about it. He felt like he talked about it all the time. In his head. To Linden. That was weird. Different and weird. He smiled at the thought.

Anokhi was waiting, so he said, "Secret? Naw, no secret. How could it be a secret if you know all about it?"

"I don't know all about it. One time I heard Peachy say something once about stiltwalking at the racetrack. But I still don't see what that has to do with running."

Albert started what he thought would be a brief explanation.

"Okay, so Peachy's been teaching me to stiltwalk."

"Mmhmm. I know."

"And he says that I have to run every day."

"Mmhmm." Anokhi paused for a second. "Why?"

"Well, see, you don't just walk around on stilts. There's some hard moves. You need muscles and . . ."

"What's so hard?" Anokhi interrupted.

Albert lifted one leg up behind him and did The Grab on his ankle, hopping up and down on his other leg.

"This! This is hard!"

Anokhi grabbed one of her legs and began hopping too.

"That's not hard."

"Yeah, well, try it on stilts one time. They're heavy! And you have to balance and not fall over. And you can't just hop—you have to stay with the music."

Anokhi, still hopping, was now gasping for breath. She panted, "Oh. I. Get. It."

She lost her balance and stumbled into Albert, who

lost his balance too. They ended up leaning against the fence and laughing, all four of their feet planted firmly on the ground.

"Good thing we weren't on stilts," said Albert.

"Yeah, I guess it's harder than it looks. How did you learn anyway?"

"Buckets," answered Albert.

"Buckets? Of what? What are you talking about?" Anokhi looked confused.

"Just . . . buckets," he said, and now she looked irritated.

"No, for true! I'm not fooling with you. I started on buckets! Just like those white plastic ones like they put out behind Selma's Café."

He pointed across the bay at Gatling Creek's only restaurant.

Albert had meant to give Anokhi her present and leave, but the words began to pour out. He told her about clomping around on buckets and how his muscles had ached at first and how hard Devil Wheel was and how his costume didn't fit. His sweat dried in the wind coming off Gatling Creek Bay as he told her about sitting in trees, sitting on roofs, about being scared and then not being scared anymore.

Anokhi's little brothers wandered up to see what was going on, got bored, and left, and still he talked. Only when Anokhi's mother called her in to chop vegetables for dinner did he wave goodbye and trot back up the hill. As he jumped onto the porch at home, he thought maybe running wasn't so bad after all.

24

Boxing Day

Albert tossed about. Between the midnight Christmas Eve service and the Christmas this morning, he should have been exhausted, but he couldn't sleep. The whole day had been strange. The house had seemed empty without Linden. The two families had always spent Christmas together at one house or the other, but not this year. Instead of the big roast pig leg and macaroni pie and dark, sour greens and cassava and all the other fixings that Mommy usually made, they'd had a roast chicken and a cake from the Sunshine. Less noise, fewer presents, less everything.

One good thing was the gifts he gave to his family. He'd never had his own money to spend on presents before, and he'd fretted over his choices. The owner of the tourist shop near the Big Island ferry dock got so tired of Albert's questions that he shooed him out the door empty-handed. Only when it turned out that he knew Daddy did the shopkeeper let him back in. It had been worth it, though.

Mommy had gone on for so long admiring the wrapping on her present that Albert had to remind her to open it. He had chosen a combination teapot and teacup that said, "We Be Jammin'" in swirly letters on the side. He wasn't sure what "We Be Jammin'" meant exactly, but the colors were pretty, and Mommy liked tea.

"Albert, honey, where did you ever get such a thing? It's perfect! I'm going to drink my tea out of this every single day!"

"It's from China. The cup goes on top of the pot like a cover! See? That way the tea stays warm."

By the time she finished hugging him and kissing him, he was glowing like Rudolf's nose.

Daddy didn't make as much of a fuss, but he gave Albert's head a rub when he opened the combination key ring and miniature jackknife, and when he read "Don't Worry, Be Happy" on the knife, he laughed and said, "That's me, Mon, that's me."

The memory distracted Albert for a moment, but then his mind charged ahead. Boxing Day, exciting and terrifying, was just a few hours away. What was the racetrack like? What if he fell? What if he messed up? And what about his costume?

He was sure he would never sleep, but the next thing he knew, he heard roosters and Mommy was shaking his arm and whispering, "Come on, stiltwalker. Wake up. I want you to eat something before you get on that ferry."

"Why are you whispering?" said Albert as he sat up and tossed his sheet to the floor.

"Ssshh. Get dressed now. I don't want to come back in and find you asleep again."

"I'm up, I'm up! What about Chente and Ashanti?"

"Ssshhh! Let them sleep. They'll take the afternoon ferry."

"What about you and Daddy?"

"We'll take the afternoon boat too. There's no sense in all of us rushing—you're the only one who has to be there early."

Albert watched from his seat by the window as pelicans dove from the gray sky and dropped clumsily into the water by the ferry dock. Mommy was right—it didn't make sense for the whole family to rush when the races didn't even start until 2 o'clock, but that didn't make him feel less lonely on the nearly empty ferry, or less nervous about what lay ahead. The window, cool against his forehead, vibrated as the big boat picked up speed. In his head, it sounded like "Can't cry, rather die."

He pulled himself away from the window. He was too old for that foolishness. He gave his shoulders a shake but his thoughts ran ahead to the racetrack. His family would be there, he knew that, but who else? Probably some Gatling Creek guys. He made a face. Not Anokhi. Definitely not Linden. He had expected Linden to phone when he arrived on Big Island, but he hadn't. Maybe he had stayed in Brooklyn after all. Or maybe he just didn't want to call.

Albert's dark thoughts disappeared when he saw

Peachy's van, Ja-Ja Jumpers in white T-shirts hanging out of every window. During the noisy, bouncy ride to the racetrack, all he could think about was how to keep from being crushed against the door every time Peachy went around a curve. He was very relieved when the van slowed and pulled into an enormous gravel parking lot. At the far end of the lot stood a wide, tall building that looked as plain as a warehouse, except for the giant red letters that spelled out "**SEA FANS RACE TRA   K**." There was no track to be seen, as the building blocked the view from the parking lot.

When the van drew closer to the building, Albert could read smaller signs that read "Grandstand Entrance," "Ticket Window," "Adults $5." Peachy veered diagonally across the empty lot toward the end of the building and parked next to a big, boxy truck that had a golden horse-shoe painted on the side and straw spilling out of the back. The Ja-Ja Jumpers tumbled out of the van like clowns from a circus car and followed Peachy to a gate in a tall fence marked "Horses Only." The guard was suspicious, but Peachy convinced them that they were the Special Boxing Day Entertainment. He swung the gate open and allowed them to pass to the other side of the fence.

Albert had imagined that the horse racing track would be like the one at the high school where Chente ran the 100-yard dash, but it looked about a hundred times bigger. The endless oval of the racetrack was carpeted in soft, dark earth. The grass in the center, still sparkling from the morning rain, was so magically green that he blinked staring at it. He walked up to the bright, white fence along the track's edge and rested his elbows on it.

A breeze carried a sweet, pungent smell from a low building at the far end of the track. A stable, Albert figured, and manure, but it smelled much nicer than Mr. Wheatley's goats ever did. He breathed in the unfamiliar odor as he admired the grass, the white fences, and the misty hills rising just beyond. But what fascinated him were the powerful horses that fidgeted and danced as they were led back and forth along the track. They looked as though they wanted to flatten out into a dead run. Their trainers gripped their lead ropes like children holding helium balloons on a windy day. They stroked the horses' necks and talked softly to them. Albert couldn't take his eyes off the huge, beautiful animals. A whack on the back got his attention.

T. J. yelled, "What are you staring at? I've been calling and calling! C'mon! Catch up!"

Peachy and the others were walking toward the grandstand, and the boys took off running after them. The grandstand seats started high above ground, and rows and rows of empty benches climbed all the way up to the corrugated metal roof. Food vendors were setting up in the space under the seats, and the aroma of cooking onions replaced the stable smell.

A man appeared near the sign that read "Finish Line" and caught Peachy in a hug. They laughed and pounded each other on the back for a while, and then the man, still laughing, looked at the stiltwalkers.

"Where's the rest, Cousin?"

Peachy answered, "You just chill, Cousin. They'll be here soon, soon. But listen, Mon, I'm looking and I don't see anyplace we can put on stilts. The grandstand roof is too high. The fence is too low. We need something—trees, low roofs, something."

"I hear you, I hear you, Cousin."

The two of them moved away, talking and occasionally pointing. When Peachy returned, he was shaking his head and laughing.

"I hope you guys had a big breakfast," he said. "You've got some walking to do. We're gonna perform here."

He pointed at the track in front of the "Finish Line" sign.

"And we're gonna put stilts on there."

He swung his arm wide and pointed at the stable. It looked very far away, and Albert groaned and protested along with the others. Peachy listened for a moment, nodding and smiling, but then he interrupted them.

"This is an adventure. Something to tell to your grandbabies. Now fetch the stilts and see if you can find Junior and the rest. Miss Ursula too."

For the next hour, there was a lot of confusion and walking from the parking lot to the stable and back again. In the end, all the Ja-Ja Jumpers were found, Miss Ursula arrived with the bag of costumes, and the stilts and costumes were toted to the stable yard. The sun had burned away the cool of the morning and was climbing in a cloudless sky.

In the paddock behind the stable, Albert waited with the other Ja-Ja Jumpers, stepping gingerly to avoid the manure that blanketed the ground. He was thirsty and hot, and the smell wasn't nearly as sweet up close. He breathed through his mouth, feeling sick and hungry, both at the same time.

He watched two horses being led back to the stable. Sweat gleamed on their dark coats. How could they race around that giant oval in such heat? Maybe he didn't have it so bad. At least no one would be sitting on his back while he performed. If he performed. What about his costume? Peachy joined them at last, along with a man in overalls.

"Ahright?" he said.

The response was a ragged chorus of "Ahrights."

Peachy clapped the man on the shoulder and said, "Otense, here, has a room inside the stable that's clean where you can put on costumes. Be careful when you come out—hold 'em high, high, and don't drag in the mud and such. Use these crates when you climb up on the roof. Ahright? Lean the sticks up along here before you go inside."

They moved to get their stilts, but Otense interrupted them.

"Hold up! Hold up! Not yet! The horses'll be coming out for the first race in a minute. I don't want you spooking them. If you want to watch, you can stand against that fence, but no flapping and no yelling, y'hear? When they're gone, then you can move around."

An announcer's voice crackled through the P.A. system. From inside the stable came piercing whinnies and the clatter of hooves on concrete. The stiltwalkers pressed against the fence, whispering excitedly. Albert forgot all about the heat and the flies. One by one, seven horses danced out of the stable, heads tossing, sometimes crab-walking sideways, sometimes bursting into a short gallop. The jockeys in their white silk pants and colorful shirts sat high on postage stamp-size saddles, their knees bent almost to their chins. Somehow, they managed to control the powerful animals.

Once the horses had left the stable, the Ja-Ja Jumpers ducked through a fence and ran in. Otense led them to a room he called the tack room. It smelled of leather. Saddles and bridles hung from racks on the wall, tall boots were scattered on the floor, and hard, black helmets sat lined up on a shelf. It was crowded but cooler than outdoors, thanks to a little air conditioner that rattled in the only window. As Peachy pulled costumes from Miss Ursula's bag, stiltwalkers grabbed them and slipped them on.

Peachy said, "Soon as you're ready, go tie on your stilts. And hold up those pant legs! Miss Ursula's in the grandstand, and if she sees manure on those costumes..."

Peachy gave the empty bag a shake and folded it neatly. Albert watched, horrified. Peachy had said he would talk to Miss Ursula. Had he forgotten? Had she forgotten his costume?

Dry-mouthed, he said, "Peachy?"

"Yeah?" Peachy was busily putting on his own costume. "What's up?"

Peachy looked up and instantly said, "Oh, sorry. Mon,

sorry, sorry. I forgot. Miss Ursula just gave me yours this morning. Now where did I put . . ."

Peachy fumbled on the floor and came up with a green plastic bag that had fallen under a bench. He brushed bits of straw off it and handed it to Albert.

"Here it is. Miss Ursula said this'll work, no problem. You ahright, Mon? Sorry I gave you a fright."

"I'm cool," Albert said weakly as he shook out the shimmering fabric.

Even in the dim room, his costume took his breath away. Oh, if only it fit. He tugged the vest on over his white T-shirt. It didn't slide off. He bunched up first one leg and then the other and stepped carefully into the long, wide trousers. The waist was too loose. He started to panic, but he discovered that Miss Ursula had added a hidden drawstring under the elastic waistband. He pulled it tight and knotted it, and then knotted it again. No way was he going to let those pants fall off. He had a costume!

Everyone else had left by the time he finished dressing. Albert hurriedly rolled and rolled his voluminous pant legs until they were bunched safely above his knees. Holding one in each hand, he made for the door. He was trying to figure out how to turn the knob without dropping either pant leg when it swung abruptly open. He jumped back, just avoiding being hit, and ended up eyeball to eyeball with a grown man who was almost as short as he was.

The man, startled, said, "Hey! Who . . . what are you . . . oh, you're one of those stilt kids, yeah?"

Albert, even more startled, just stared.

The man waited, then chuckled and said, "I guess you never saw a jockey before, yeah?"

Albert found his voice. "Well, I saw those guys on the horses just now, but not, I mean, not . . ."

"Not on the ground? Yeah, it's like that for most folks. They see us on horses, we look one way. Yeah. One way. On the ground we look different."

He looked Albert up and down and shook his head.

"Looks like you're gonna be growing some more. Too bad. Yeah. Too bad."

"Um, too bad?" Albert managed to say, still clutching his pant legs, staring at the man as he bustled around the room.

"Yeah. You'll never be a jockey. Yeah. You'll never be a jockey. Too bad. Yeah."

Albert didn't want to be a jockey, never had, but the sympathy in the man's voice was so sincere that he felt for a moment as though he might be missing something. The man began to polish a pair of boots, humming to himself. He's happy, thought Albert. Happy to be short. The idea was as startling as the little man himself.

"I'm Jockey John. Yeah. Jockey John," the man said.

"I'm Albert. Are you in a race today?"

"Yeah. Two races. Yeah. Two," he said with a smile.

At the sound of footsteps on the roof, Albert said, "Uh-oh. I better get going. I hope you win. Um . . . could you open the door, please?"

Jockey John pulled the door wide and Albert, still gripping his rolled-up pants, waddled out.

Jockey John's forehead wrinkled in a worried way as Albert passed, and he said, "You watch yourself now. Those stilts are dangerous. Yeah. Dangerous."

Horses leaned their big heads out over their stall doors to watch Albert walk out of the stable. Even their heads were gigantic. Jockey John was about to climb up on one of those wild beasts, and he thought stilts were dangerous. Albert was still smiling as he clambered up on the roof.

T. J. greeted him crankily, "Where were you? Your stilts are over there," he said, pointing. "And watch out when you sit. This stupid roof burned my butt."

Albert noticed that others were sitting on sneakers and flip-flops while they tied on their stilts. Hopping painfully from foot to foot as though he were on beach sand in August, he managed to take his sneakers off, sit down on them, and dangle his legs over the edge of the roof. He licked his palm where the metal burned it and began wrapping foam around his legs. T. J. wasn't the only one who was cranky. Everyone was wilting in the heat.

"I'm thirsty."

"I'm hot."

"I'm starving."

Peachy pulled the last knot tight on his stilts and pushed himself clear of the roof. As he stood, the legs of his costume fluttered down and the rags and the foam rubber and the rough wood disappeared.

He stood facing them, side-to-side stepping for a moment, and said, "Hot enough for you?"

There were as many boos as chuckles at the terrible joke.

He ignored both and went on. "It's hot for December, for true. I think the sun came out just to watch you dance. And it looks like that old sun's not the only one who came out."

He pointed past them, and they all turned to look. The grandstand was packed. A shiver of nervous anticipation raced up Albert's spine. Two girls screamed and everyone started chattering loudly. Albert could tell he wasn't the only one who got a scary thrill at the sight of all those people.

Peachy watched them, chuckling, and then said, "Ah-right?"

This time, "Ahright!" came back to him loud and clear.

The mood had shifted from cranky to giddy.

"After all that rain, even in the sun, that track'll be a little soft," Peachy went on. "As soon as your stilts are on, take a walk around here in the paddock, get used to the soft ground."

Albert tugged impatiently at his rag ties, and then stopped himself. Wing nuts.

He took a Peachy breath and counted out loud, "One, two, three, four. One, two, three, four."

Everyone else was already on their feet, but he did more Peachy breaths and made himself be calm as he untangled the rags and tied his stilts firmly to his shins. He pushed up and started cautiously pacing around the paddock. The stilt tips sank alarmingly. Peachy was right. This was harder. A rumbling sound came from the grandstand and grew into a roar.

"That must be the end of the fourth," said Peachy.

Otense answered him, "No, Mon, third. Two more to go before you're up."

The sweating stiltwalkers slowed down at that news.

Otense watched them for a moment and said, "Anybody thirsty?"

He disappeared around the corner of the stable and returned tugging the end of a hose.

He handed the nozzle up to Peachy and said, "No fancy bottles, but it's better than nothing."

They passed the nozzle around. Albert thought he had never drunk anything as delicious as those first gulps of rubbery-tasting water. T. J. squirted water on his heavy braids.

"Ooooh, that feels gooooood!" he said and shook his head wildly, sprinkling everyone near him. Others grabbed for the hose, and by the time the fifth race was announced, they all were soaked and laughing.

When the crowd roar died down at the end of the fifth, the Ja-Ja Jumpers' laughter did too. They got busy fixing hairdos and retying stilts.

Once the last horse had returned safely to the stable, Peachy said, "Ahright! Show time!"

He swung one stilt and then the other over the fence and began walking along the racetrack toward the grandstand, and the stiltwalkers followed. Peachy's pace was so slow that it made Albert feel as fidgety as a racehorse being held back by its jockey.

Junior blurted out, "Peachy, hurry up, Mon! We're never gonna get there."

"We'll get there, we'll get there. I'm just giving all those folks a little time to forget about the horses and get excited about us. And besides," he chuckled, "it'll give the costumes a chance to dry."

A cooperative breeze, hot but refreshing, had picked up, and the thin fabric was drying quickly. Pant legs rustled and flapped in the wind. The buzz of voices from the seats grew louder.

"Hear that?" said Peachy. "They've noticed us now!"

The announcer's voice came back on, talking excitedly about the Special Boxing Day Entertainment Surprise.

"That's us," said Peachy. "We're the Entertainment Surprise. Ahright. Now let's pick it up!"

They walked faster. Albert felt less nervous the more he had to think about swinging his stilts into longer strides.

"Spread out now! Swing your arms!" called Peachy.

They did as they were told, and it seemed that Peachy was right about giving the audience time to get excited.

By the time the announcer said, "Ladies and gentlemen, put your hands together for Big Island's very own Ja-Ja Jumpers!" he could barely be heard over the clapping and cheering.

Just as they got to the finish line, the Ja-Ja Jumpers' own music came blaring through the powerful speakers, louder than they'd ever heard it before. They stopped walking and started dancing, lifting their knees high, as smoothly and easily as they had at practice. Peachy turned to face them, his back to the crowd. The Ja-Ja Jumpers waited for his signal.

When the next song came on, Peachy grinned and shouted, "Ahright!"

The Ja-Ja Jumpers fanned out and each swung a stilt in front, held it up with both hands, and began playing air guitar on the upraised stick. The audience laughed with delight.

Albert could hear the names of other stiltwalkers being called out from seats, but nobody yelled, "Go, Albert!"

When the music changed again, a faster beat, they took turns moving through their routines, sometimes dancing, sometimes clowning. Some did The Grab and danced on one leg. Some did Road Race: They lined up, bent forward, almost doubled over, and pretended to run a race, kicking their stilts up high behind but staying in one place. For The Ballroom, Junior and T. J. made a big show of bowing low and inviting Shirleen and Katesha to dance, and the two couples waltzed like elegant, very tall grown-ups. Some did The Fall, pretending to tip over backward until the crowd gasped in horror, and at the very last second springing up to standing again. The audience laughed and applauded. When the music stopped, there was a groan of disappointment.

Someone handed Peachy a microphone, and he turned to face the grandstand. The stiltwalkers were confused— they hadn't rehearsed this—but they stood patiently, step-stepping, while Peachy told the audience about their Friday night practices and hard work and good grades.

When he said proudly, "These kids, these kids right here, these kids are Mocko Jumbies for true!" they peeked at each other, smiling sheepishly, surprised and flattered. They were even more surprised when he began introducing them to the audience. He said a name and a form in school, and one after another they stepped forward, pleased and embarrassed, and bowed and waved and grinned. The entire grandstand seemed to know every stiltwalker, and the cheering went on and on.

Albert felt hot, then cold, then hot all over again as he waited for his name to be called, nervous that he might mess up his bow. As the wait grew longer, he grew more nervous thinking that Peachy had forgotten him.

Finally he heard, "Last but not least, here's the newest Ja-Ja Jumper. He doesn't even go to high school. He's Albert Quashie, and he's in First Form at Penn Scoville Middle School over on Little Scrub Island."

Albert's cheeks flamed and he felt dizzy. Somehow his legs moved him forward and he bowed as he'd seen the others do. He didn't mess up. The grandstand was a blur of color and noise, but as he straightened up from his bow, a movement caught his eye.

Someone was leaning over the grandstand railing above him waving wildly and screaming, "Albert! Yo, Albert, Albert! Hey! Hey, Albert!"

He didn't recognize the oversized New York Yankees shirt or the wrap-around reflecting sunglasses or the black do-rag, but the voice was unmistakably Linden's. Albert wanted to whoop back, but the music for Devil Wheel came on. He managed a little wave before he was swept into the finale. He couldn't stop grinning. Linden! Linden was here!

He threw himself into the fast-moving Devil Wheel steps. When the other Ja-Ja Jumpers began The Grab, he dodged into the center, just as they had rehearsed. He waited for the music to cue him and then he danced his heart out, running, spinning, and hopping around the circle. He could have danced for hours, but the song ended. The Wheels dissolved and the Ja-Ja Jumpers, both stilts back on the ground, held hands in a line facing the grandstand. Albert moved with them as they bowed repeatedly to the cheering crowd.

25

Good News

The applause followed them back to the stable. The Ja-Ja Jumpers clowned and kicked as they walked away to make sure people kept clapping. Albert felt as though his stilts were made of balsa wood, as though he could run around the track as fast as any racehorse.

At the stable, he pushed and shoved with the other Ja-Ja Jumpers as they rushed to grab a spot on the roof and laughed just as deliriously and screamed "Ouch! Ouch! My butt!" just as loudly, as they were painfully reminded how hot the sunbaked metal was. Otense was ready with the hose, and they drank and squirted and splashed. They jabbered like thrasher birds as they untied their stilts.

"We're the best! We're superheroes!"

"We're better than that! Peachy called us Mocko Jumbies!"

"Did you hear that clapping? I thought I was gonna go deaf!"

"Hey, T. J.! Even you didn't mess up! Not even once!"

"We're famous now, for true! We're superstars!"

"That was so cool when Peachy said our names. Hey, Peachy, how did you find out all that school stuff anyway?"

Peachy smiled as he looked up from untying his stilts, but all he said was, "Watch it! Watch it, Superstars! Take it easy getting down."

The bubble of excitement began to deflate once the Jumpers shouldered their stilts for the long walk back to the parking lot. They couldn't walk on the track because races were going on—they had to stumble through uncut weeds and brush outside the fence. The stilts were heavy, the sun was hotter than ever, and thorns scratched at their legs.

In the parking lot, they wearily hoisted the stilts onto the roof of Peachy's van and tied them down. Peachy stowed the costume bag and other odds and ends in the van. Albert felt sad watching him. It was as though he was doing it for the last time.

He slammed the rear doors shut and looked slowly around at each Ja-Ja Jumper. His voice was somber when he spoke. "Ahright? You all should be proud of yourselves. You guys are Mocko Jumbies for true. I'll tell you something—Big Island is never going to forget that show. Not ever."

He stopped talking and looked around again. *Was he saying goodbye? No more stiltwalking?*

But Peachy grinned his widest smile and said, "Good news. You get to do it all over again. The Ja-Ja Jumpers are going to walk in the Big Island Easter Parade!"

200

The Jumpers dissolved in screams of astonishment. The Big Island Easter Parade. Everyone—everyone!—came to watch it. Boxing Day was nothing compared to the Easter Parade. They screamed themselves hoarse.

As they quieted, Peachy said, "Ahright! Ahright. I guess you know there'll be other Mocko Jumbies there. Some from Trinidad. You'll be the youngest ones, but you can still be the best. We've got some work to do, so I'll see you on Friday, ahright?"

Albert stood staring up at the wall of faces that rose above him. He was alone—the other Ja-Ja Jumpers had scampered up the stairs and evaporated into the grandstand. He didn't see a single familiar face. How was he ever going to find his parents? Or Linden.

Then he heard "Albert! Albert!" and saw Chente, Ashanti, and Linden racing toward him. They were on him in seconds, fist-bumping and back-slapping and shoving and yelling, pulling him up. At the top of the steps, people in the seats turned to stare at them. Chente noticed and pointed at Albert, hollering, "That's my baby brother! He's a Mocko Jumby!"

Linden kept saying, "That was so cool! That was so cool!"

Ashanti said, "Move it, Albert. Mommy said to fetch you right away. See way up there? See, she's waving? That's where everybody's sitting. Let's go."

"Everybody?" asked Albert, but Ashanti and Chente were already leaping up into the grandstand.

Albert and Linden followed more slowly. Linden draped his arm across Albert's shoulder, just like always, talking breathlessly, nonstop, into his ear.

"That was cool, Mon! So cool! You're a stiltwalker. You're a Mocko Jumby. That is crazy cool. Y'know, they have this thing in Brooklyn, they call it a Caribbean weekend or something. It happens every year, like Festival here, or Easter, only bigger, with Mocko Jumbies and everything. You're just as good as those guys! Better! That thing at the end where you were dancing around all by yourself?"

"Devil Wheel," Albert piped up.

"Devil Wheel? Yeah. That was amazing!"

Albert and Linden were abruptly interrupted by "everybody." It looked like Mommy had invited everyone she knew and, judging by the baskets and coolers, had prepared more food than they could ever eat. Linden's parents were there with the Big Island aunts and their families. Red Dog and Granny Quashie and even Miss Alice were there. There were people from church and neighbors from the settlement—they had taken over a section of the grandstand and turned it into a party.

Mommy caught him in a tight hug.

"My baby! I was so scared I couldn't breathe! How did you ever learn to do that?"

In between words, she planted kisses all over his face. He saw Ashanti laughing at his embarrassment as he tried to wriggle away, and gave up and laughed with him. He was pushed from person to person, patted and hugged, kissed and congratulated. Red Dog didn't move, but extended a long, slow arm out to Albert.

As they bumped fists, he said, "Look at you, Mon. From roadie to rock star. Just don't forget us little people."

The racetrack speakers squawked harshly as another race was announced. People in rows behind hollered at them to sit down, and Albert escaped to the end of a row. He made a face as he scrubbed at his hot, kiss-wet cheeks.

Linden landed next to him with a crash, his arm across his shoulders again, and said, "Hey, you okay?"

"I'm hungry, that's all."

Mommy must have read his mind, because as soon as he spoke a heavy plate was passed to him from behind. He pulled back the foil and aromatic steam filled his nostrils.

"Chicken roti! Wow! Thanks, Mommy!"

He waved down the row to her.

He heard Daddy call out, "Dig in, Albert," as he passed along a bottle of Ting. "You need to keep up your strength if you're going to be stiltwalking, so."

Albert dug in, washing down bites of savory stewed chicken with gulps of Ting. A plate was passed to Linden, and they ate in silence for a few moments.

Loud laughter made them look up. Mommy's party was getting a little wild. Sammy was drumming on a plastic cooler and Leonard was standing on his seat and dancing with Miss Ellie, who was in the row above him. Mommy and Linden's mother were in the center of the noisy crowd, hugging and swaying to the music.

Albert and Linden looked at each other and at the

same instant said, "Crazy people!"

Albert giggled. He and Linden had been saying "crazy people" about their parents since they were little, often at the same time, and it still made them laugh. They fist-bumped, and Linden began talking again, this time about his plans for the rest of their holiday. Go fishing in the dinghy. Dive for conch shells in Josiah Bay and sell them to tourists at the ferry dock. Climb Kestrel Peak and camp overnight. Albert, who had forgotten what it was like to be swept along by the tidal wave of his friend's plans and schemes, nodded and grinned contentedly. Just like always, he thought, as he scooped up the last trace of gravy with the last bit of soft flatbread, but better.

"And you know what else?" Albert said.

"What?"

"I'll teach you to stiltwalk."

"Really? Wow! Okay. Cool! Teach me quick, quick. If we sell conch shells while we're on stilts, then we'll really . . ."

"Hey, Little Man!"

Albert looked up and his smile faded. Above him, feet planted wide, arms crossed, stood Silton Stevens. Albert still wasn't sure how angry Silton was at having Albert for a tutor. Was he about to find out? Still holding his plate, he rose awkwardly to his feet and turned to face him. He didn't know what to expect, but when Silton moved it was to extend his fist.

He smiled and said, "That was cool, Little Man. Really cool."

Albert returned the bump with his free hand and

mumbled, "Ahright, Mon."

As Silton walked away, Albert sank down into his seat, surprised and very relieved.

Linden said looked up from his plate and said, "Little Man? What? Oh, I get it! Because you're so big when you're up on the stilts. Cool nickname, Mon! I like it."

Albert just smiled.